# DIVINE DESCENT

## DIANA MARIE DUBOIS

Cover art by Anya Kelleye  www.anyakelleye.com

Cover photo by Jean Maureen Woodfin Model: Tionna
Petramalo

Edited by Maxine Horton Bringenberg and Beth Lake

Formatted by EmCat Designs

# DIVINE DESCENT

DIANA MARIE DUBOIS

This book is dedicated to Amanda, my new sister. Thank you for giving me a second chance at life with your gift.

# ACKNOWLEDGEMENTS

To all my readers thank you for being patient with me on this book. The last two years have been hard for everyone. I went through my second kidney transplant and the pandemic hit soon after. But I finally pressed on and got this one done. A final shout out to Anna Leach, thank you for being a new reader. I hope you enjoy the actions of my characters and that the stakes were high enough.

# GLOSSARY

**Baron Cimitiere**- The gate keeper of the fourth gate. He is the guardian of the cemetery, protecting the graves. He wears a tuxedo with tails and a top hat. His taste is expensive. Even though he is just as crass as the other Guédé, he shows polite manners and an upper-class air while doing so.

**Baron LaCroix** – The first gate keeper of the gates of Guinee. He is often seen wearing a black tailcoat and carrying an elaborate cane. He is the ultimate suave and sophisticated spirit of death - quite cultured and debonair.

**Baron Samedi** – The keeper of the seventh gate of Guinee. He is the loa of the dead and is the last loa a spirit sees upon their death. He is married to Maman Brigitte.

**Guede Babaco** – Gate keeper of the those who did them wrong.

**Guede Nibo** – The second gate keeper of gates of Guinee. Formerly human, Guede Nibo was a handsome young man who was killed violently. After death, Baron Samedi and Maman Brigitte adopted him. He is envisioned as a nasal dandy. Nibo wears a black riding coat or drag. When he inhabits humans, they are inspired to lascivious sexuality of all kinds.

**Guede Plumaj**- The gate keeper of the third gate of Guinee.

**Voodoo** - Louisiana Voodoo, also known as New Orleans Voodoo or Creole Voodoo, is an African diasporic religion which originated in the U.S. state of Louisiana

The gates of Hell are open night and day; smooth the descent and easy is the way.

-Author: Virgil

# Prologue

## *Rosie*

My eyes glazed over and fell to the ring on the ground—the one Julian had given me asking me to spend the rest of my life with him. Without thinking I scooped the pink diamond into my hand. But as I replayed the last things that had happened, all I saw was Julian and Ares disappearing into the ground. The tears burned my eyes as they poured down my cheeks.

Still on the ground, I scraped at the cement, trying to get to them. "Come back!" I screamed so loudly my voice grew hoarse. My father picked me up, but I flailed in his arms, screaming, "No!" I thrashed and pushed from his hold on me and ran back to the spot I'd last seen Julian. I placed my palms down on the ground, feeling the heat, my nails jagged and broken from trying to claw at the ground.

I felt the warm presence of my Guardian beside me. I faced her with tear-stained eyes and pushed my face into her soft fur. "Athena, he can't be gone. This is the final chapter; my heart can't take another loss." I wrapped my arms around her body and sobbed uncontrollably.

"Mom, everything will be okay." She nuzzled me with her nose.

My father nudged me gently to get my attention. "Don't worry, we'll help you find them," he coaxed me, rubbing my back.

All I wanted was to get away, so I struggled under his grasp. "Let me go now," I hollered, spittle flying from my mouth.

"Calm down, Petal."

At the sound of the nickname, anger bubbled up, threatening to burst out. "You don't have the right to call me that," I sneered, only now wanting my mom. She would know what to do. Deep down I knew I was lashing out because I was in pain, but I didn't care. I wanted everyone to hurt.

"Rosie, I meant no harm," he whispered.

His empathy caused me to stop being a spoiled brat. I gaped up at him and reached for his hand. "Dad, I need to get him back." Resolve now replaced my tears.

"We'll discuss it later—please let me help you."

Hesitantly I nodded my head. I walked the few steps toward him and leaned against his body. Exhaustion took over and stopped me from doing what I needed to be doing. My eyes became heavy. He lifted me into his arms, and I held onto his strong body.

Dad carried me into the house. I glanced over his shoulder one last time, looking at the spot where Julian and Ares had disappeared, the gas lanterns now lighting up the courtyard as the sky darkened. Even though I knew others were in my house, I paid them no mind.

Dad put me back down on the floor. "Do you think you can walk?" he asked me.

"Yes," I mumbled.

Athena leaned against me to brace me. My legs started to feel like jelly as we made our way to my room.

My body and heart ached. My dad pulled back the quilt on my bed and I plopped down on it, then scooted and rested against the pillows. He helped pull up my quilt and I tugged it up to my chin. Athena gently jumped up beside me, placing her head on my lap.

The door creaked open, and Miss Alina peeked inside. "May I come in?"

I nodded, not knowing how my head was able to move. It felt like it was packed with rocks. She smiled and walked in. "Here, Rosie, I brought you some tea. Drink it it'll help you relax." She placed the mug on my nightstand.

Tears still trickled down my face as I snuggled deeper under the covers. "I don't want to relax. I want Julian back."

She sat down beside me on the bed, brushed a strand of my hair back, and tucked it behind my ear before holding my face in her hands. "Honey, we *will* get him back, but we need a plan. Now drink, please."

I opened my hand and the ring sat in my palm. Staring at it, tears slid down my cheek. Mrs. Alina wiped them away and took the ring, placing it on my nightstand.

"Please drink, Rosie. You need rest."

Hesitating for a second, the look on her face finally encouraged me to take her suggestion. Carefully I picked up the mug, the warmth and steam rising instantly relaxing me. As the cup met my lips, I drank the soothing liquid. It slid down my throat coating everything it touched. All my tastebuds were satisfied with the unknown herbs I could not place. Soon my eyelids grew heavy, even before I could put the mug down.

"What bib youv giben me?" The words stumbled out slowly, incoherently.

"Don't worry, my child. Just sleep."

Miss Alina took the mug from me, and she and my father left the room.

The door clicked shut and I tried to open my eyes but

couldn't. Slinking down further in the comfort of my bed, I could still feel the tears flowing, in no danger of drying up anytime soon. Snuggling up to Athena and succumbing to my mystery tea, I sighed deeply and let myself fall asleep.

*A few hours later*

My eyes opened and I looked at the clock. It was midnight. My gaze fell on the silver ring with the pink diamond on my nightstand. It sparkled brightly under the light of my lamp, beckoning me to remember what had happened last night. It had been hours since the demon had taken Julian and Aries.

Athena remained curled up at the end of the bed. Even though I sensed she wasn't asleep, she kept quiet. A sigh escaped my mouth. Afterward I muttered, "Why?"

Without saying anything, she comforted me by inching closer. I sat up in bed with a jerk, my toes barely touching the hardwood floor. My matted hair fell in tangles in my face. I brushed a strand away and tucked it behind my ear, but it refused to stay in place. Swiftly I picked up a hair tie from off my nightstand and wrapped it around my hair and made a messy ponytail. Not quite up to my mom's standards, but she wasn't there so I did my best.

For a few minutes I stared at the ring, and suddenly I scooped it up. It cut into my skin as I clenched it tightly in my palm. The cold metal brought more tears to my eyes, but just slightly. I chuckled softly and spoke. "Guess I'm all cried out, huh Athena?"

With the ring clutched tightly in my hand I rolled back onto the bed, relaxing on my back. I opened my hand and held the ring up. It glistened in the soft light of my room. Then I slipped the ring on my finger and held my hand up.

Athena lifted her head up, crawled over to me, and softly placed it on my chest. "What are we going to do?" she asked.

"We're going to go and get him, that's what we're going to do." The words flew out of my mouth with reckless abandonment. "Come on, let's go!"

Swiftly, I scooted out of bed and went over to the dresser where my jewelry box sat. My hand went instinctively to the top drawer, where my bracelet, amulet, and voodoo doll were. I took them out and laid them on the dresser.

"These things will protect me. They hold love, made by those that loved me and are no longer here." I turned to Athena and smiled sadly. "Next we need to make sure we bring the necessary items for offerings to the loa."

Athena jumped off the bed and padded over to the trunk where I kept bottles of rum, boxes of cigars, chocolate, and other items in case of an emergency. She nosed the lid up and started going through it.

"Athena, did you find anything good?" A nervous laugh escaped my mouth.

She pulled her head out and in her mouth was a box of cigars. The dog placed it on the floor. Next, Athena dug out a bottle of rum, careful not to drop the glass bottle. As I filled a backpack with enough offerings for each loa, she stepped back onto the bed. As her huge head rested on her paws, hanging off the edge of the bed, I returned my attention to the trunk, then to my dresser.

"Do you have everything?" Athena asked in a bored tone.

I looked over at her and smiled. "I just need to get dressed."

Athena picked up her big head and said, "Hurry, we need to get out of here before the others know what we are up to."

I glanced over to my French doors and could see darkness still shrouding the sky through a crack in the curtains. "You're right, it will be light soon."

I tugged open the second drawer and pulled out clothes. Quickly I shoved my legs into a pair of worn jeans and slipped an old concert T-shirt over my head, smoothing it down my body. I shut the drawer quietly, then I slipped the chain with the amber jewel around my neck, stuffing it inside my shirt, letting the amulet fall against my chest. Soon the coolness of it had warmed against my skin.

A sigh escaped my mouth as I picked up the bracelet from Jahane and clasped it around my wrist. "Gosh, I miss her so much," I mumbled under my breath. "She would back me up on this endeavor."

I turned to face Athena and stuffed my voodoo doll into my front pocket. Athena sat staring at me. "Let's go," I whispered, fearing my dad would hear.

Scooping up my backpack and shoving it over one shoulder I nodded to Athena. She gently hopped from the bed. For a big dog, she was masterful at being quiet when she needed to be. She knew to be careful and not make noise.

Slowly I opened the door, afraid it would creak. But as soon as we stepped out of the room, my dad appeared in the hallway. For a slight second, I felt like I was back in time when I snuck out to meet Jahane for the nighttime parade. I hadn't seen this man growing up, yet he looked at me as my mother had that night.

Feeling the urge to roll my eyes, I stopped mid-roll, knowing I was too old for that and pushed Athena forward. "I don't want to argue."

He followed me to the living room. "Rosie, I know what you're planning. It's too dangerous." His tone was firm.

Stopping mid-step, I faced him. "No, you can't come in here after all this time and invoke your fatherly right." My voice raised to an unusually high octave, even though I knew his disappearance hadn't been his fault. But still...

"Damn it, Rosie." He slammed his fist down on the table, causing the legs to bounce off the floor. "I don't want to lose you after all this time."

My eyes narrowed as I glowered at him. "Well, I don't want to lose Julian—he needs my help."

"Can't you wait until I can get the covens to help you? Miss Alina has gone to get the others. She's working on a plan," he begged.

"No!" I exclaimed, causing Athena to wince. She dropped her head and put one paw over an ear and glanced up at me. I turned to her. "Sorry, Athena."

"It's okay, Mom."

I lowered my voice and spoke to my father. "I can't. I have only seven days to rescue him, and who knows how fast that demon can travel? Besides, I've already lost time with Miss Alina's tea," I grunted.

He stood in front of me and tried to convince me by adding, "You know Gabriela is still out there, and I'm sure her anger with you is erupting."

I pushed him out of my way. "I don't care." My words came out through gritted teeth. "She can come at me." My eyes narrowed. "And I'll kill her like I did her mother." My fists tightened at my sides. The house shook a bit from my anger.

My dad sighed. "You're more like your mom every day."

When I reached the door, I placed my hand on the knob, but before I twisted it, I turned around. "Yes, and she would understand why I have to do this."

"Rosie, I'm not her." Sadness laced his voice.

A crackling sound sprang around me, and before I could step outside, I slumped to the floor. The last thing I remember seeing before my eyes closed was my father standing over me. My anger grew, and god help him when I woke up. My retaliation would be a strong force not even he could get out of.

# CHAPTER ONE

## *Julian*

### First gate of Guinee

My heart ached, watching sadness spread across Rosie's face when the shadow demon sucked me underground. The air rushed around me as I descended below ground. When we stopped, I realized we were standing in a cemetery familiar to me. Ares stayed closer to me.

Before me stood Marie Laveau's tomb. But what caught me off guard was a ghostly figure I noticed in the distance. "Who's that?" I wondered aloud.

The huge blue dog sniffed the air. "Julian, she's a spirit guide," Ares spoke to me, a sure sign that he'd started to bond with me.

Surprised at this revelation, I squinted, trying to get a better look at her, since I'd never actually seen one. Her flowing skirts swayed around her as she floated here and there. I caught a glimpse of her face, and there was sadness etched across it. *I wonder who she's waiting for?* My mother used to talk of them, but even after all I'd seen this was new to me.

"Oh shit!" I exclaimed. Memories flooded my head as I remembered my mother saying the only time they came out was to help someone get through the underworld.

An evil laugh stopped my thoughts. "She's not for you. You are my bounty, and my bounty alone." The demon grinned.

"Then who—?" But before I could finish my thought, I knew. *Crap, she's here for Rosie.* I knew nothing would stop Rosie from coming after me. But she needed to do it correctly this time, or she would be in the same predicament, and I wouldn't be here to save her. I needed a way to leave a message for her. "I can't have her coming down here for me, Ares."

"Julian, you know as well as I do her fate is already set," the dog barked out.

"Enough!" The demon demanded. "You aren't doing anything except going where you deserve to be."

A door seamlessly opened in the plaster. What I saw surprised me. Instead of seeing what I thought would be bones littering the floor, a tunnel appeared, lined with gas lanterns.

"After you." The demon waved me inside with a maniacal smile.

I hesitantly took a step forward, but not before I glanced one more time at the spirit guide. The demon kicked me in the back of my legs to get me moving, causing me to stumble, but I caught myself. The inside appeared much bigger than it had from the outside.

"Hurry now, before someone sees us and wants to follow," the demon growled.

I hesitated before stepping inside. As soon as I was in, the door to the mausoleum creaked closed, until the last crack of light had been extinguished. One by one the lanterns flickered to life, lighting the tunnel with tiny red flames. The small blazes cast a red hue along the dark passageways.

A fear of falling into a black hole of nothingness grabbed me. Ares grabbed onto the back of my shirt as my feet contacted dirt. I caught my balance and steadied myself by grabbing onto the dirt-covered wall.

Up ahead, gas lanterns continued to line the walls of her tomb, lighting up as we walked. The scent of death and decay permeated my nose. Ares sneezed. "Bless you," I told the dog. My gaze returned to the room we stood in. Amazement crossed my face.

The demon smiled at me. "You're a lucky human—most don't get to see this when they are alive. You can appreciate the beauty of where you are." He grinned widely, showing off a mouth full of nothing.

My observation fell to the dirt-covered ground. A single coffin sat in the middle of the room. I meandered over to it and brushed a hand across the marble sarcophagus.

The demon laughed. "What did you expect, the usual heap of bones? No, only one person has the right to this tomb, and her bones are well hidden from people that may want to disturb her afterlife."

"You mean she's not buried here?" I continued to trace the marble—the intricate designs were beautiful.

He cocked a brow at me. He tapped his lips with a bony finger. "Yes, well not really." He suddenly grew angry and muttered, "You, boy, do not have the right to know the answer to that question." He faced me as I turned to look at him in disgust. "Hurry up. we're wasting time."

The demon pushed me again, and I fell down the proverbial rabbit hole. Gravity took hold of me, and the closer I got to the bottom I saw dozens of bones and skulls littering the ground. Then I landed with a thud onto the death and decay. My hands dug into the dirt, and I shivered as one of my fingers went into a fresh eye socket of a skull.

"Ugh." I wiped the decaying flesh from my hand, then braced myself. When I stood, I glanced around to see walls of dirt and tree roots. "Where are we?"

"We're at the first gate to Guinee." He smiled giddily as if we were on one of those haunted tours in the city. "I'm your host, Ailred," the demon said. "Follow me." He spoke graciously as he finally introduced himself to me.

Ares stayed close as we followed the demon. All of a sudden, I felt a pain deep in my gut. I doubled over, clutching my stomach. The agony wouldn't stop. "What's happening to me?" I said through clenched teeth.

"Julian, breathe through it," the Warrior spoke.

I glanced at him while trying to quell the pain. Taking a deep breath, I slowly let it out. After a few more breaths I regained my composure and stood up. The discomfort subsided some.

My attention returned to Ailred. "Where are you taking us?" I asked with curiosity.

He turned and faced me. "No more questions. Just move." He pulled me forward.

"I want answers." My feet stopped in their tracks, and I managed to pull from his grip. But before I could speak again, a figure emerged from the shadows.

"Who dares to enter?" The voice spoke, chilling me to the bone.

Ailred bowed to him. "I've brought payment for the witch's indiscretion of coming down here in the wrong order." He chuckled eerily.

I tried to focus my eyes and saw a figure who looked a lot like Baron Samedi, except for his stature. Thank god for Rosie teaching me some things about the loa.

He tipped his stovepipe hat and grinned. "I'm Baron LeCroix. And you are?" He leaned back against the side of the tunnel. Boney hands reached out to him and grabbed at him, but he paid no attention. Then, as his gaze fixated on me, his eyes went wide with knowledge of who I was. I stared at him agape. Black eyes sat in the alabaster bone sockets. I couldn't pull my eyes from his.

"This is—" Ailred began.

Baron LaCroix interrupted him. He stalked over to me. "Ahh, the Rougaroux." He smiled, leaning closer to me. But he didn't touch me.

His putrid breath choked me, and I leaned on Ares for stability. The creature continued to sniff me as I stood there. With his mouth inches from mine, my eyes teared up at the scent of his wretched breath.

"Yes," I stammered out. "How do you know who I am?"

"Because he knows all. He's an incarnation of Baron, as are all the barons guarding the gates. The guedes though, you will meet used to be humans." Ailred looked at me as if I'd just fallen off a potato truck, but happy with himself for relaying the information.

Baron LaCroix ignored him and looked down at my hands, before letting out a chilling laugh. "Boy, that ring won't be of any use to you down here." He shook his head in disbelief. "It really won't stop you from turning into what you are." He laughed. "I presume that when Marinette gave you this bauble, she never knew you'd be down here." He eyed me with a quizzical expression.

Unconsciously I twisted the wolf head around on my finger. A wave of heat emanated from the ring, but I was careful not to show the discomfort. "What do you mean?" An uneasy feeling settled in my stomach.

He leaned back with one black boot on the moldy wall, nonchalantly inspecting one bony finger. "The rules down here don't apply to the ones up there." He pointed upwards. "If you get angry—" He stopped before I could interject. "I know that's what makes you turn." He grinned but continued. "You'll turn into that thing you hate most." He pushed away from the wall and inched closer to me. He draped a boney arm around me. "Why do you wish to rid yourself of such a beautiful transformation?" His smile was eerily giddy.

As I backed away from him, I bumped into the dirt wall behind me. "Because I don't want to turn. I don't want to endanger those I love," I replied matter-of-factly. The scent of death and decay wrapped around me and choked me. Skeletal hands reached out, caressing me. I knocked them off and moved away, just as one tried to pull me into the wall.

Baron LaCroix chuckled loudly. "Well, it appears that's no longer any of your concern." He waved his hands in the air. "This will be your new home." He chuckled then changed the subject, and asked, "Do you have an offering for me?" He grinned and held out his hand.

Panic ensued but Ailred nudged me. "Here, give him this." He handed me a box that appeared out of thin air.

I handed it to him and watched him unwrap the black box. The baron flipped the top open to reveal a pack of cigars. He reached in with a long alabaster bone finger and removed one. He raised it to his face and placed it under where his nose would have been and sniffed.

"Ares, do you think that is good?" I was not entirely sure the dog would know.

The loa smiled. "Yes, Julian, this is satisfactory. But I hope your demon host has more because you will need an offering for each gatekeeper."

My head spun to Ailred, who was digging a long finger in his ear. I shook my head in disgust.

The loa cocked his head at me and glanced down at my hand. "Just one more thing. I'll have your ring as well."

"But...."

He sauntered back to me. "You no longer need such baubles."

Before I could answer the ring disappeared and now sat perched on LaCroix's boney finger. He held his hand up, grinning wide, and admired his new trinket.

"Perhaps this will be sufficient for now. You may

proceed to the next gate. But be careful of them." He disappeared in a puff of gray smoke, his voice lingering as he continued to laugh.

"What did he mean?" I asked Ailred, but he ignored me.

Up ahead the dark tunnels were immediately lit up by gas lanterns, much like the ones in the city, though these balanced in midair and swung above our heads as we made our way to the next gate.

# Chapter Two

## *Rosie*

As I woke up a wave of anxiety washed over me. My gaze went over to the curtains. The dimness of dusk peeked through them. "Shit, shit, what day is it?" I glanced at the clock. Almost a whole day had passed since my dad had bespelled me. "Athena, wake up, wake up." I nudged her hard with my toe. "We need to hurry and get out of here."

She rolled over, her jowls hanging open. "But Mom, your dad doesn't want you going."

I cocked an eyebrow at her. "When have you ever known that to stop me, or us for that matter?"

She sat up and cocked her head. "True. Then let us go save the flea bag and my brother."

Holding back laughter at the old nickname for Julian, I scooted out of bed. "First I need the perfect spell so my dad can't stop me this time." I clapped my hands together.

Athena jumped off the bed and went over to the desk. She grabbed my spell book and brought it over to me.

"Thank you," I said as I patted her head.

I flipped open the book and pulled the pen from the middle where it was nestled. With the pen in hand, I tapped it to my lip, then grinned, coming up with the perfect spell. After seeing the words come to life dripping in dragon's blood, I raised my arms and said the words.

*Powers above, powers that guide*
*Hear my words from far and wide.*
*Unseen I must stay as I make my leave.*
*My presence here he must believe.*

"Now where is my backpack?" I wondered out loud and scanned my room. "Come, Athena, it must still be in the living room." I waved her over.

"Let's just hope your dad hasn't gone through it," she barked out.

I chuckled. "No chance of that. I put a spell on it so only we can see the contents." I pressed my ear against the door. "Do you hear anything?"

"No." The dog shook her head, flinging drool all over the place.

"Thanks," I said, wiping the slobber from my arm.

I peeked out of the door and held my breath. Carefully I stepped out of my room and tiptoed down the hall. Even for Athena's size, she was able to keep her noise level down. But that was short-lived as she skidded into me, knocking me over, causing a loud ruckus. "Oh no!" I screamed, then hastily slapped my hand over my mouth as I sat sprawled along the hardwood floor. I tossed my hair back over my shoulder and looked over at her.

"I'm sorry, Mom." She looked abashed.

I held my breath, waiting for my dad to come out any minute, but he never did. "The spell worked." I stood and dusted myself off. "Let's hurry." I saw my bag over by the door. Quickly I scooped it up and we headed out the door.

As we walked through the crowded streets, I noticed the bright moon above me. It wasn't the normal orange of a blood moon, but a deep crimson instead. Even the bright lights of the city tried in earnest to outshine the orb in the sky. But nothing would undo the eerie red glow. It peeked from between two buildings, leading me down the street as if it knew just where I was going. When we reached the cast-iron gates of St Louis Cemetery No 1, I stopped. I continued to follow the moon and opened the gates, making sure to be as quiet as possible, but to no avail. It creaked loudly, making it known to everything dead or alive in the cemetery that we were there.

"Hurry, Athena, before we get caught," I whispered, pushing her inside and quickly shut the gate. This time it did so with less noise. The moon popped in and out of the trees, begging me to continue to follow. Up ahead stood the first gate to the underworld, enshrined in a glow of red haze. The blood moon positioned itself right above it like a beacon, beckoning to me with unabashed authority. I stepped forward a few steps, holding onto Athena's collar with a tight grip. An eerie sensation crawled up my spine, making me shiver slightly.

"Mom, you're choking me," Athena coughed.

"Oh, I'm sorry." I let go of the grip, stopped, and looked around.

The dog stopped walking. "What's wrong?"

"Nothing. I think someone's following us." I looked around.

She started to growl. The hair rose along her back. "I'll rip them apart."

"Shh."

She stopped and sniffed the air, then sat on her haunches. "It's Marie Laveau."

"How—?"

But before I could answer my own question, the voodoo queen appeared from the shadows beside me, her hair tightly pulled up in a chignon. She wore a flowing red skirt and a white blouse.

"Where are you two off to tonight?" she smirked. "Especially on this night of all nights." She waved a hand toward the red moon in the sky.

"To save Julian." But I stopped suddenly. "Wait, what night of all nights?"

"Why, it's All Saints Day, my dear child, and we have a blood moon to boot."

"How could I have forgotten?"

My mother and I always celebrated it by helping clean the graves for others. She would always leave fresh flowers on those that showed signs of having no visitors. Visions plagued my memories. I shook my head—I wasn't going to go down that road. I had to save Julian.

"Well, that isn't going to stop me."

I tried to stalk off. She stopped me by placing her hand on my shoulder. Slowly I faced her, but held my breath, knowing she would try to stop me.

"I don't think that's wise." Her expression was sad. "Today of all days, the gateways are the most active, as are the loa of the underworld."

I tugged from her grip. "Good, it'll be easier to enter." The determination was evident in my voice.

She shook her head and looked off into the distance. "I fear you're in danger. Especially with the added blood moon in the sky."

"I don't care. I'm saving the man I love."

"Please be careful. If it was just the All Saints Day it would be different. But with the added blood moon, the loa will be even more demanding."

I nodded. "I'll be careful."

She let go of my shoulders. "You know you'll have to enter each gate in the right order." She smiled genuinely.

I dropped my head. "Would you tell me the correct

order?"

Her finger nudged my chin, then she tipped it upwards. "I'll do better than that. I have someone there at my tomb to help you on your journey."

"Are they already waiting for me?"

She nodded.

"You knew I would be coming?" I asked in disbelief.

She chuckled lightly. "I'd heard rumblings of Julian being brought down to the underworld."

"You knew—" I began, my anger raising in my voice, but her look stopped me suddenly.

"I do not mess with the underworld unless Baron Samedi requires it of me, and since he didn't, I let it go." She took my face in her hand. "Besides, I knew you'd be here to reclaim him. Nothing will stop your determination for those you love. Now, since you're still intent on going to the underworld, I need you to retrieve something from each gate for me." She eyed me with a slight grin. I felt a wave of bewilderment cross my face. Her eyes lit up and a smirk appeared on her face. "You knew one day I'd ask you for a favor."

"But I must focus...." I was afraid to tell her that my main concern was Julian, not getting little tokens for her.

But she must have read my expression. "Rosie, what I must ask of you is, I know, perhaps dangerous, but you owe me." She sounded concerned. "Besides, it's for Marie Laurent." She sounded a bit worried.

I gasped. Last I'd heard she'd been sent to help the fairies. "I'll do what I can to help you."

She smiled, and something told me she wasn't telling me the whole truth.

"I need to meet each loa anyway." I smiled.

"Good." She smiled and handed me a slip of paper. "Don't let them know you are taking anything, dear."

"But how will I get them then?"

She winked. "You're a witch—I'm sure you can come up with a spell. But you'll have to do one without your notebook and pen. We don't want those spells getting into the wrong hands." She smiled.

I unfolded the paper and read it. Beside each name of the loa in Marie's fancy handwriting was a specific item to get in detail.

Baron Lacroix tiny skeleton with red stones.
Guede Nibo egret feather
Guede Plumaj mummified chicken foot
Baron Cimitiere Queen chess piece
Guede Babaco tattooed skull
Baron Kriminel severed head
Baron Samedi skull from his staff

After reading I folded it and stuffed it into the back pocket of my jeans.

"No, no, Rosie. Commit it to memory, dear child."

I tugged it back out and read it a couple of times until I could recite it over and over.

"Good." Marie Laveau touched the piece of paper and a tiny flame extinguished it.

# Chapter Three

## *Julian*

### Second Gate of Guinee

Up ahead I saw it, and it was exquisite—the wrought iron gate. Once we were closer, I could see the designs. Tiny skulls adorned it, dancing and then stabbing each other with swords. Blood dripped and trickled toward the glass doorknob.

Ailred placed his hand on the now red handle and opened it, then nodded for me to go before him. The moment I stepped through the gate I experienced a horrible pain that crawled up my spine and shot out to my fingers and toes. I almost stumbled down the steps but caught hold of a railing made of what I could only guess were bones of the dead. My grip made me wince, but I didn't dare let Ailred know. He stopped and turned around. To not alert him to my misery I grinned.

"Coming," I said.

I regained my composure and took deep breaths.

When the pain subsided, I continued down the stairs with Ares following me

As Ailred and I continued moving further down, the reality of what I had gotten myself into came crashing around me. The demon remained quiet on our trek. We continued walking down a dark tunnel where hands were reaching out, trying to grab us. I swayed out of the way of skeletal fingers that brushed against me, trying to pull me into their grasp. The further we went down the more the scent of decay stung my nostrils.

Up ahead a dim light illuminated the ground. I blinked once, then twice, trying to focus my eyes. Soon I could see that the ground was encrusted with blood that had seeped into it.

Ares kept close to me, practically leaning on me as we kept our pace. "I won't ever leave your side," he spoke only to me.

"Who enters?" a nasally voice spoke from the dark.

I looked around, trying to see who had spoken, but nothing. As we walked further, we were met by a young man in a black riding coat. He leaned on a tall black staff with a cigar perched between his first two fingers. He flamboyantly stalked towards us.

Ailred bowed, then stood straight. "Ailred here. I'm bringing Julian—"

The demon's tone was hard as he interrupted him. "Ah, I'd heard the rougaroux was here." He smiled.

"How'd he know?" I whispered to the demon, who just smiled.

"They all knew you were coming here. In fact, I was saving this for later." He stopped, then his grin turned almost clownlike. I shuddered as he continued to smile. "You're something of a treasure down here. Even though your ancestors have followed this same path, your dual nature is something special. We would love to have your ancestor who started the line, so what's better? You, a witch and a rougaroux," he sneered.

"I'm sure that's true, but I have not mastered my

powers, nor am I sure I have any."

He glared at me. "I have to disagree."

We were interrupted by the man walking over to us. He offered me his hand. "I'm Guede Nibo. The loa and keeper of the second gate to Guinee." He waved his hand in the air as he pranced on his toes around me, tipping his staff here and there. He reminded me of the skeleton man from *The Nightmare Before Christmas*, but with a body of a man. He brushed back long dark dread-locked hair.

My eyes grew accustomed to the dark, and I could see what looked like a stage and seats to either side of a red-carpeted walkway. Turning my focus back to him, I said, "You aren't like the guard of the first gate."

Ailred began to speak, but Guede Nibo stared at him. He laughed, then spoke in a nasally tone. "What I'm sure the demon was about to say is, unlike the other loa here, I was once human. My murder was extremely brutal, and Maman Brigitte and Baron Samedi took me and made me a loa and bestowed upon me the honor of guarding the second gate."

"This must be a bad dream," I muttered under my breath.

Ailred glanced at me and guffawed. "No, it isn't."

The dancing loa continued his movements, though now he was gyrating his hips sexually. He thrust his hips at me, then draped his arms around my shoulders. "Why don't you rid yourself of this lower-level demon," he inclined his head at Ailred, "and stay with me?" he hissed out seductively. Ares growled low and the loa jumped back, screaming in a high-pitched note.

I waited for him to stop. Once he had I smirked and crossed my arms over my chest. "I can't. I need to pay a debt," I said sarcastically.

"Well, you can blame that on your girlfriend, who dismissed our rules down here and did what she wanted to," Ailred said in a disgusted tone. He then tugged my arm, obviously irritated. "We should get going."

"Wait, don't you have an offering for me?" The guede waggled a finger at the demon in admonishment.

"Why must we give offerings to every loa if I'm taking him to die?" Ailred snorted in disgust.

Guede Nibo stopped prancing and stared sternly at the demon. "It does not matter what you are doing, you must still give an offering. Now look who's trying to bypass the rules," he spat sarcastically.

The demon materialized an offering out of thin air and handed it to him. "Now we must get going," he blurted angrily.

Ghede Nibo glared at Ailred, who slunk back in fear. The loa grinned eerily. "Maybe Julian would like to see Rosie."

"Is she here?" I looked around for her.

The loa burst out with laughter. "No, but she's close." He trailed a skinny cold finger across my face. I shuddered in response to the touch. "Please stay and watch." He draped his arm back over my shoulder and walked me down the red-carpeted runway.

Now I could make out more of the scenery. On either side sat what looked like an audience in chairs. In fact, every chair was filled with people—no, the dead. Some were skeletons, while others still had skin on their bones. Their lifeless bodies sat waiting for a show.

"Who are they?" I pointed to them.

Guede Nibo laughed. "Why, the audience, of course."

He walked me up to the front and onto the stage. A chair appeared underneath me, pushing me to a sitting position. Ares sat beside me, placing his head on my lap.

"Well, damn it all to hell," Ailred grunted, but stood off to the corner, pouting.

A red curtain pulled back on either side, ropes magically tying them out of the way, and then the curtain behind slowly rose, revealing a hazy scene. It shimmered in and out until it remained clear. "Watch." The loa placed a hand on my shoulder as he sat beside me. The coldness of his touch caused me to shiver. I tried to shrug it off, but he wouldn't budge.

I sat still and waited. I gasped as Rosie came into view. She stood in front of the tomb, the same one I had—though it was no surprise since she was friends with the owner. Out of the corner of my eye, I saw a figure float over to her. I leaned forward, reaching a hand toward the veil. When I did, it rippled at my touch, and then Rosie looked straight at me.

"What the...?" I exclaimed.

The veil disappeared before me and once again I stared in disbelief. The curtain slid down, hiding the veil behind it.

"No touching. That's enough," Nibo said.

I turned to face the audience. They remained still in their seats. "Perhaps this show wasn't meant for them," I pondered.

"You are right, Julian. They are here for the next show."

Guede Nibo stood, his chair disappearing. "I give you permission to pass through to the next gate. It's beyond the curtain," he indicated with an outstretched hand.

# Chapter Four

## *Rosie*

### First gate of Guinee

After leaving Marie, I followed the moon to her tomb. My nerves rattled as I stepped up to the mausoleum. A figure emerged from behind it.

"Hello, Rosie." A friendly voice got my attention.

"Um, hello," I stammered. "Who are you? Are you the one Marie told me about?"

"Yes." She walked over to me and touched my hand. "I'm Shay, your spirit guide. I'll guide you through the gates of Guinee"

"Wait." Athena stepped between us and sniffed her. Her nose covered every inch of the woman. Instead of walking around her, she stuck her nose through the ghost's body, her head sticking out the other side. It curved around and she grinned at me. "Okay Mom, she's good. I don't smell anything bad about her."

Shay shimmered as Athena pulled her head away

from her.

I grinned at the woman. "Sorry about that. She has a mind of her own." I shrugged my shoulders and held my arms out.

The dog sat on her haunches and cocked her head at me. "It's to protect you."

Shay laughed. "It's all right. I had already been warned by Marie." She smiled and patted the dog on her head.

"She's something special, and I wouldn't go anywhere without her." A wave of comfort wrapped around me.

She waved her hand in front of the door to the tomb and it opened. "First I have one rule to share with you. Be careful of each gate. They are alive, and if touched could be dangerous."

I nodded, not entirely what she meant by being alive.

"We should really get going if we want to save your loved one." She glanced around a strange expression etching across her ghostly face.

I followed her gaze and had that earlier eeriness crawl up my spine again. "Is someone out there?" I wondered aloud.

She shrugged her shoulders and held her hand out to me. "Shall we go?"

I stepped forward through the opening, which revealed a lighted tunnel. I stopped and turned to Athena. "Do you think you can sense Ares or Julian?"

She stood tall and still, her nose in the air. "No Mom, something's cloaking his scent."

"Damn it." I looked over to Shay. "Sorry."

"No worries. I'm afraid the underworld may mess with her senses. We'll find them." She started to walk toward the tunnel. "Be careful, the next step is a doozy."

I walked a few feet then fell forward, screaming as I continued. Athena tumbled after me. As we kept falling, my life flashed before me like a movie being played on the dirt walls surrounding me.

Before landing I closed my eyes and reached out, touching the dirt-encrusted walls on either side of me. My hands gripped at the filth. I prayed to the witches before me and called out for the roots to stop me and Athena. The ground rumbled and sent its sinewy tendrils out to me. The vines reached out, gently stopping us from our tumultuous descent. We slowed and touched down lightly to the ground. My feet touched the earth. Athena landed softly as well. Shay floated above us.

Gas lanterns bobbed and balanced above us, leaving a hazy light around us. I looked around and saw what looked like a cement spiral staircase. "Are we going down there?" But before Shay could answer we were interrupted.

"Hello, young witch." The voice startled me since I couldn't see where it came from. "I'm Baron LaCroix. What brings you to my home?" A man—no, a skeleton man, a smidge shorter than Baron Samedi but with a top hat on his head—walked out from the shadows.

Nervously I cleared my throat. "I've come to ask permission to pass to the next gate, please."

He tipped his hat at me and bowed. "Why do you want to pass?"

"I'm in search of my boyfriend." I crossed my arms in defiance, daring this loa to stop me.

He walked closer to me, his gold-coated staff in hand. He leaned forward and smiled a toothless grin at me. "Why don't you stay here and forget this other man?" He thrust his hips toward me."

I smiled kindly so as not to offend the baron and spoke. "I'm sorry, but I must decline your offer."

He smacked his mouth where his lips should have been, making a clacking noise with the bones. He eyed me. "Then do you have an offering for me?" he asked.

"I do." I dropped the backpack and Athena dug around in it. She pulled out a box of cigars.

He held out his hand. "Just what I love."

That's when I saw the tiny skull with two beautiful red stones as eyes dangling from his staff. There was my first item for Marie. But something else also caught my eye. I gasped, then covered my mouth with my hand. Julian had been here, and this loa had something of his. I shook my head as a fearful thought entered. I silently spoke to Athena. "Julian's been here—the loa has his ring." I sucked in a deep breath and inaudibly said a quick spell.

*In this moment my hand be filled*
*Words I speak magic willed.*
*In it hides a stone the deepest red.*
*Now I hold the head of a wolf and the skull of the dead.*

As I handed him the box the skull and ring appeared in my hand. I peered into my bag, where they nestled deep down into a secret compartment. I glanced at him quickly to make sure he hadn't noticed my thievery.

He ignored me as he ripped the purple ribbon from the box and tossed the lid to the ground, which swallowed it up.

"May I pass?"

He took one of the cigars and reached up to a lantern and lit it. "I'll give you a bit of advice, Rosie. Don't stay down here any longer than you must. Also, don't die down here, or you'll remain here forever in whichever gate you expire in." He smirked.

Athena sat and her tail brushed against the floor back and forth, stirring up dust and god knows what else. "Mom, does he know where Julian is?"

Baron LaCroix glanced down at the dog and grinned. "The dog talks?" It wasn't really a question he wanted answered.

She cocked her head to the loa, then back to me. "He can hear me?"

His laugh bounded off the walls around us. "Of

course, I can. It's much different down here than it is above. The same rules don't apply." He walked over to the dog. She never flinched when he reached a skeletal finger out and touched her. "Oh, you're something unique. There was another just like you here a while ago."

"Julian was here?" I exclaimed, causing the loa to drop his cigar.

Athena nudged it gently with her nose. LaCroix picked it up and stuck it back in the void that used to be his mouth.

His black eyes sparkled. "You're looking for the rougaroux?"

"Yes," I replied hopefully.

"Then that is why you stole back his ring?" He smiled. Before I could reply he shook his head. "Oh yes, I know all. Besides, you may need it more than I ever did." He paused. "If what's been fated is to come true."

I choked, then cleared my throat. "What is supposed to happen?"

He shook his head. "No, I can't speak of it. You and the rougaroux must find your own way. But you must hurry." He waved us away, but his voice echoed as we left. "Be careful, young witch. Guinee is not a safe place."

Shay waved me forward. "Rosie, this way." She inclined her head down the stairs as I stood there trying to make my feet move.

"What's with the cryptic message from the dead?" I wondered aloud to no one in particular.

"I don't know, Mom, but we must find Julian." Athena nudged me as we descended the staircase. I held onto a railing and shuddered at the thought of what my hands touched, but put it out of my mind.

# CHAPTER FIVE

## *Julian*

### Third Gate of Guinee

Stepping up to the stage, I pulled back the curtain to see another wrought iron gate, this one somewhat different. The tiny skulls adorning it this time wore feathered masks. The skulls battled and the blood seeped into the doorknob and turned the glass red. Ailred placed a hand on it turned it then we walked through. As the gate banged closed behind me one of the skeletons reached out and poked me with his sword.

"Ouch!" I hollered in pain. I rubbed my arm and then instantly fell to my knees.

"Why are you whining?" Ailred said. "It was just a little poke." He smiled mischievously.

The pain emanated up and down my spine. Nausea hit me and the contents of my stomach came out with a lurch. I wiped my mouth on my sleeve, and after a couple of deep breaths, I finally stood.

I glanced at the demon, who eyed me with hatred and discontent. He turned away from me, yelling, "Hurry up."

I planted my feet on the ground. "Julian, what are you doing?" Ares barked.

"I'm not going any further until I get to see Rosie again," I demanded loudly, causing Ailred to turn around. But I couldn't move any further as I doubled over in pain. "What the hell is happening to me?" I choked out.

Ailred glowered as he stalked toward me. He went to grab me, but I growled, feeling the hair crawl up my arm, covering it from shoulder to wrist.

"Uh, Julian." Ares nudged me anxiously with his head. "You're shifting."

"I know," I growled, watching with a close eye on Ailred. "Show me," I snarled, my voice becoming gruff. The vibration of drums caused me to turn around and glance into the darkness. "What is that?"

"Guede—" Ailred started to speak but was hastily interrupted.

"I'm Guede Plumaj." The man stepped from the shadows with a swagger and moved around me with an air of pretension. "What or who do you wish to see?" He cocked his head.

As soon as the guede spoke, the hair retreated down my arm. I shook my body, suppressing my urge to return to my rougaroux form. "I want to see Rosie. I want to make sure she's all right."

The guede's eyes lit up. "The witch is here?"

"You know of—" I started to speak, but Ailred interrupted me.

"Yes, she's following him," he hissed, glancing back at me with a sneer.

The loa looked at me. "Well, I think I can oblige you this little thing. I so look forward to meeting her," he said in a giddy tone. "But first my offering."

Instead of looking at me, he focused on the demon

beside me. Ailred conjured up a bottle of rum and handed it to him.

"Thank you." Then he waved his hands in the air and a shimmering veil appeared.

I blinked my eyes a couple of time and tried to focus in the darkness. Before my eyes, Rosie appeared. I reached out to her, but the veil between us was strong. The guede shook his head. "No touching," he growled.

I pulled my hand back and rested it on the back of Ares. Rosie, followed by Athena, walked down a long dark tunnel.

"Where's she going?"

"She's on her way to the second gate," Plumaj spoke.

I knew I had to hold off moving on, so maybe she could catch up to us.

It was like a silent movie playing before me. She looked scared, but at least she had Athena with her. Then another figure appeared beside her. I recognized her from earlier when I was topside. Her hazy appearance seemed to disappear and reappear. "Ailred, why is that woman with her really?"

He squinted closely, then mumbled under his breath.

"Answer me." I turned and faced him, demanding an answer.

He eyed me, then dragged me away from Plumaj. Through gritted teeth, he angrily spat, "Do not ever speak to me like that, and especially in front of a loa."

"Then answer my question," I demanded.

He sighed loudly like a petulant child.

"Julian, be careful in trusting a demon. Remember, they lie." Ares's voice lit up my head.

The guede interjected before my demon captor could speak. "A spirit guide's job is to help people with their transition from the living."

"But Rosie isn't dead." My panic screamed out through my words.

"My dear boy, she's here to help Rosie on her journey through the gates. You know, to go through the gates correctly." He smirked. "It seems as if she has very powerful friends up there." He leaned closer to me. "Without help, a person could easily get lost down here."

Ailred found his voice, interrupting and grinning evilly. "She may be dead soon, though." He grabbed me by the shoulders.

Guede Plumaj interrupted. "You know," he tapped a skinny finger to his chin, "maybe I should keep you here with me."

"And keep my bounty? No!" Ailred screamed.

"But why not?" He toyed with the demon. He eyed me with a smirk. "Julian, you know you will eventually have to die to remain here."

I wondered what the guede was getting at. What kind of fresh hell was this? "How long before I die?" I asked him. Fine hairs erupted along my arms and I controlled myself, although it was difficult, to stop turning. The hairs disappeared as fast as they'd appeared.

"It depends, but I'm assuming when you get to the last gate. Baron Samedi will take you to the other side."

My thoughts swam through my head like a tidal wave. I had to make sure Rosie wouldn't be harmed. But how? I pondered.

Plumaj leaned against the wall, grinning in amusement. Skeletal hands reached out, but he paid them no mind.

"I need more time." I wrenched myself from Ailred's grasp and inched as close to the veil as possible without touching it. I sucked in a deep breath and watched as Rosie rounded the corner, one that looked familiar. "No Rosie, don't leave," I hollered. But she couldn't hear me.

"That's enough." Ailred dragged me off.

Ares bounded up to him and clamped his huge jaws around the demon's arm, causing black ooze to drip from it. He screamed in horror as his arm smoked from the bite. He shook it wildly, but that just made the smoke thicker. "What have you done to me?" he screamed like a little girl.

I may have stopped to laugh at the situation, but I had to get away from him. As Ailred rubbed at his arm I made a sudden escape with Ares close at my heels. "Come on, Ares." We turned corner after corner, not considering we could get lost. After the last corner, I skidded to a halt and bent over, trying to catch my breath. "For a demon, he sure is a pansy," I finally breathed out, and leaned against the dirt-encrusted wall. I dared not look at what I'd actually rested on, since I swore I heard it breathe.

Ares sat on his haunches and cocked his head. "It's not his fault. Something in our DNA burns them. We should get going though." He nudged me.

Then a thought popped into my head. "What if we get lost and are doomed to walk around here forever?"

"I should be able to get us where we need to be— or we can just wait for Rosie here," Ares said with confidence.

"No." I shook my head. "Ailred may find us."

"But it's possible I could shroud us in secrecy."

"You can do that?"

"For a bit, yes, to keep him off our trail."

But before Ares could do his magic, we heard Ailred hollering for us. I pushed off from the wall. Down one dark tunnel after another we both headed, Ailred's voice following us, echoing in the distance.

As we rounded another bend I told Ares, "We need to find—" But before I could finish, I came face to face with the demon.

Ailred glared and grabbed me by the throat. He leaned in and his putrid breath invaded my senses. "You shouldn't have done that. And as for your dog, he'll get his karma." His lips curved upwards in an eerie grin. "You'll never escape again," he sneered.

In seconds he had a rope. As he let it go, it dangled

in the air. Two little skeletons appeared and danced with it, each one holding an end in its hand. Not once did their little bodies strain to hold up the rope. Before I could jerk back, they had restrained my wrists. I pulled back, but one of the tiny skeletons shook his head while shaking a bony finger at me. They leaned their alabaster heads back and laughed.

"Julian, try to use your magic," Ares spoke to me.

But I couldn't move. It was as if I was glued to this spot. I watched the skeletons as each one took a sword, performing a macabre scene. One of them took his head off and held it like a shield to the other one, the toothless grin mocking the other one. I stood there in shock as the scene unfolded before me. Then with a jab, the skeleton shoved the sword into the other one. The head in his hand fell and rolled around in the air. I watched in fascination as its eyes stared at me. Its body slumped over, clutching its chest, then went limp. Tiny droplets of blood landed on the ropes, and they tightened around my wrists.

I shook my head and dislodged the stupor I was in. "Run, Ares!" I shouted, but it was too late. They had tied a rope around his neck. He bucked and thrashed under the strain of the ropes. "Don't hurt him." My voice was full of anger.

"As much as I wish they would, your dog is protected by magic," Ailred grumbled. "But this will stop both of you from trying to escape," he continued, disdain coloring his words.

"How did they bleed?" Curiosity stained my question.

He laughed coldly. "They're part of Baron Samedi. It keeps you tied to the underworld."

I refocused my attention on Ares. The little skeletons once again performed the scene, and when they were done, they writhed around in the air dying until they turned to ash and floated away.

Despair wrapped its ugly head around me as I stood hunched over. But as quickly as it hit me, a wave of anger coursed through my body, and I looked up at Ailred. Course hair began to cover my body and I growled lowly. "Don't you know who and what I am?"

He laughed, barely glancing over his shoulder. "Yes, and you and your family don't scare us down here."

"You should be scared." I lunged at him, but he raised a hand and stopped me.

"Julian," Ares called out to me.

The monster tried to take hold of me, but at the sound of Ares, I quieted. With all my might I pushed the monster part of me away. The hair started to recede, and once again I was a man.

# Chapter Six

## Rosie

### Second Gate of Guinee

Before us stood a wrought iron gate with tiny, decorated skulls adorning it. I watched as a macabre scene unfolded before me. As they died, blood oozed along the gate and down to the glass doorknob. It was stained in red. I reached forward, grasping it, and turned. On the other side, I waited for the others to follow.

Athena sauntered through. I heard a cackle. "Hurry, Athena." A tiny skeleton climbed up on the top of the gate. "Watch out, Athena!" I screamed.

She tucked her butt and tail in just as a tiny skeleton reached out and tried to touch her. It screeched in anger. Athena turned around and growled. The skeleton scampered back onto the gate and flipped a bony finger at my dog.

I laughed and petted her. "Next time be careful. I

couldn't bear for anything to happen to you."

Shay floated through and I figured she was safe from the horrible gate. "From here on we'll be traveling down deeper into the earth," she told us.

I followed Shay down the cement steps. Athena remained close, almost leaning on me. Thank goodness for my Guardian. Her proximity always made me calm. As we descended the steep steps, my hands slid across the dirt walls, then into something sticky. "I will not scream, I will not scream." I kept repeating the mantra until I reached the bottom.

Finally, we reached the last step. I released the breath I hadn't realized I'd been holding. "Where are we now?" I breathed out. I looked around and blinked my eyes, trying to get them accustomed to the semidarkness. In the distance, I saw a tiny light, but it quickly disappeared.

Shay shivered a little as she looked around. I looked out, seeing three different pathways. "The trail should be this way." She pointed to the left.

"Which one, though?" I asked, worried we could take the wrong one.

She looked at me with a blank stare.

"Are you sure? You don't seem sure," I blurted out.

"It changes each time I come down here, and I want to make sure we take the correct route because if not, we could be stuck down here for eternity."

She paused and closed her eyes. With her hands outstretched I remained silent and let her do her magic to find the correct way. As the silence became unbearable, I let my mind open to my surroundings. When I did, I could hear whispers around me. So much noise from the dead.

From somewhere in the distance, I heard water. Athena sensed my unease and leaned into me. I waited patiently for Shay to open her eyes, yet I still heard the voices of the ones who were destined to remain here.

Suddenly Shay's eyes opened, and she smiled. "This way." She started walking down a path. Her feet made no impressions in the ground. Athena and I hurriedly followed.

"Shay, can I ask you a question?"

"Sure, Rosie." She smiled at me.

"How did you die?" I asked meekly, not wanting to offend her.

"It's a long story. Maybe I'll tell you when we have time."

I nodded, leaving it at that. Silently we meandered down a dark path only lit by Shay's ghostly figure. The gas lanterns above us swayed but held no light. I couldn't take the darkness any longer. I touched my amulet and it began to glow around us.

When we came to a dead-end, my heart plummeted to the souls of my feet. A wave of sadness crept around me. "I thought this was the way."

Before she could answer me, a figure materialized from the dirt wall.

"Rosie, you are going to have to learn to trust me." Shay turned around and smiled at me.

A man shimmied toward me in a black coat, his eyes dark as coal. He did a spin, and suddenly he wore a purple evening gown, with purple pumps to match. I watched him in amazement. The wall had disappeared, showing off what looked like a nightclub of sorts.

The man sashayed toward me "I'm Guede Nibo. How may I help you, Rosie?" He bowed, offering me his hand in a friendly gesture.

By now I was used to everyone knowing my name—it didn't even faze me. I took his hand. It wasn't cold or warm to the touch—it was nothing.

He led me into the room, lit only by red flamed candles. On further inspection on either side were round tables with chairs. On each table sat a single red rose in a glass vase. The dead sat at the tables drinking. I let go of his hand and smiled meekly.

"Guede Nibo, I ask permission to pass to the next gate."

He tapped a painted fingernail to his lips as he

pondered. "First, do you have any offerings for me?"

"Yes." I flipped open my bag and reached nervously inside. When I pulled my hand out, I held a bag of pistachios and handed them to him. Then afterwards, I brought out a bottle of white rum. "Here." I offered it to him.

He took the gifts and smiled a toothless grin. "Before I let you pass, may I ask you a question?" The glint in his eyes showed me he already knew the answer. "How is it that you come here to the underworld when you aren't dead?"

Standing in front of this effeminate creature, I thought how best to answer without offending him. "A demon has taken someone close to me and brought them here."

He leaned in, the smell of decay permeating my nostrils. "Is that so?" He breathed out. I choked and held back the urge to vomit from the scent of his breath.

I nodded and placed a hand over my mouth and breathed through my nose.

"Rosie, what has your loved one done to be brought down here?"

Again, I knew he already knew the answer. He was testing me.

He continued. "I'm assuming he's not dead either." He arched his brow.

I sighed and shook my head. "I came down here...." I paused, but he finished for me.

"You didn't go in the correct order, did you?" He stood and waved his hands in the air.

"No, but in all fairness, Baron—" I stopped, not wanting to say anything bad about the loa of the dead.

Nibo eyed me, then smiled creepily. "Say no more. Baron Samedi is a trickster—everyone knows it."

Athena nudged me. "Can we go yet?" she asked, exasperated.

"Wait," I spoke so no one heard but her.

I glanced up at Nibo and he bowed to us with a

gleam in his eyes. Then I saw it, the bright white feather—it nestled deeply in his bright colorful wig.

"You may pass but be careful." He chuckled. "You don't want to end up dead before you find your beloved." He held out his hand to me. "This way, dear Rosie." He led me down the red-carpeted runway, and the audience raised their glasses to me as I passed, smiling toothless grins at me. Before he let go of my hand Nibo asked, "Are you sure you don't want to stay for the show? It will be the best one to date."

"I'm afraid I have to decline. I must really be getting to the next gate."

Guede Nibo bowed at the waist and waved his hands in a circular motion. "Good day to you, Rosie." He turned and danced away.

Before we left, I silently said another spell.

*In this moment my hand be filled.*
*Words I speak magic filled.*
*Long neck, strong wings, chest so bold.*
*Egret feather my hands now hold.*

I hurriedly clenched my fist around the feather and tucked it into my backpack. Guede Nibo turned back to me. "No reason to steal from me, Rosie. I'd have given you the feather if you'd have asked." Nibo grinned down at me.

"I...uh...," I stuttered, but I didn't get a chance to apologize since he disappeared in a flash. All the dead were gone and the tables were empty—even the roses were no more. The lights dimmed and then darkness surrounded us.

Once the crackling of his disappearance had dissipated, I glanced at Shay. She stood with her arms crossed, shaking her head.

"Please don't anger the ones who guard the gates."

I shrugged my shoulders. Who would have thought he'd figure it out?

She pursed her lips. "Rosie, they know all down

here."

Quickly I pushed Athena behind the curtain, where another gate stood. The macabre skeletons danced in gyrating movements along the wrought iron. The same scene spilled out as before. Quickly, before one of the dead decided to touch my hand, I turned the crimson glass knob and the gate swung open with a creak. We hurried through and then descended another set of steps.

# CHAPTER SEVEN

## *Julian*

Despair had taken hold of me as Ares and I followed Ailred. "I'm sorry I got you into this, Ares," I sighed.

He turned his huge head to face me. "It was my choice to follow you. Also, I wouldn't give up hope if I were you. I sense that is what he wants," the dog barked at me.

A chill ran up my spine and I shivered. Solemnly I trudged behind the demon, waiting for the next shoe to drop, so to speak. Corner after corner we turned, my hands still tied together, also bound to the rope tied to Ares. Then I saw two figures standing in the middle of the tunnel. I blinked but couldn't get a good glimpse of them.

"Get out of the way," Ailred demanded.

"We can't, we're here to see him." They pointed at me.

"Who are you?" He growled.

As I inched closer to them, I recognized them. "Mom, Dad?" I asked in disbelief, my feet carrying me to them.

"Yes, son." The woman walked over to me, her face just how I remembered it.

"Are you really here?" I asked.

"We are." She chuckled.

Ailred stared at them, then at Ares and me. "No, it's not them," he screamed and ran toward us. But it was too late. She reached up and gently touched my face. "Your father and I have missed you so much." Her lips began to tremble. As she touched me, the ground dropped from below me.

"He's my bounty!" Ailred's words were shrouded in darkness as we disappeared.

The rush of air swirled around me. "What the hell!" I exclaimed. But when I opened my eyes, my feet were still planted on the very spot where I'd stood before she touched me. I looked down and saw the ropes crumble to threads. I brushed the remnants off me, and Ares shook his off as well.

"What the hell just happened?" I wondered. "I thought they could not be undone."

Ailred screamed, "You can't have him! He's mine," through gritted teeth.

Ares remained by my side as the woman tried to touch me again. I shrank back from her touch. "Who are you really?" I asked, my tone reserved.

"I'm your mother." She smiled and reached out to touch me again, but I backed further out of her reach. "What's wrong?" She smiled but her face changed for a millisecond. Her motherly façade changed to one only nightmares could describe. I shook my head, not believing what I'd just seen. The face of a beast replaced the one resembling the mother I remembered from growing up.

"Julian, that's not your mother." Ares nudged me.

"I know, but who, or what, is she?" I silently spoke

between gritted teeth,

"No idea, but don't let her touch you again."

"Why? What happened?" The questions came out loudly, causing everyone to stare at us.

"You disappeared."

"I did?"

Before I could get a glimpse of our surroundings a cold hand touched my shoulder, but this time I grabbed Ares's collar. When we stopped spiraling out of control, I looked around for Ailred, but he was nowhere to be found.

Ares followed my gaze then leaned on me, something I'd witnessed Athena doing to Rosie. It was their way of protecting us.

"Where are we?" I demanded.

"Home," the two entities said in unison. I looked around and we stood in my childhood home. The staircase stood before me. The floors and walls were freshly painted, just as I remembered them

"All right, stop it, this is beyond weird," I remarked.

The man walked over to me and put an arm around my shoulder. I tried to shrug it off but to no avail. "Look, Julian, your mother and I have been waiting for you."

"Have you?" I questioned.

"Yes. Now why don't we get out of here?"

I eyed him not trusting him. "Where to?" I questioned.

"Why home, where else?" His voice wasn't recognizable. His anger grew and then his eyes turned crimson red, as did hers.

"You aren't my parents," I shrieked.

They tried to grab me, but Ares stepped between us, growling. He snapped at one, latching on and drawing blood. He let go as the black oozed from my fake father's arm. The fake mother tried to touch Ares, but he diverted her touch and took her leg into his mouth, tearing it from her body. She hobbled and they both screamed in pain.

As the demonic figures screamed in agony, clutching at their nonexistent body parts, their true selves were shown. Black silhouetted bodies swayed back and forth as their red eyes looked around in panic. They withered away, and their screams echoed in the tunnel.

After they had disappeared my ears still rang from all the screaming. I waited a little bit more until I couldn't take the silence any longer.

"What now?" Ares asked.

"We need to find Rosie and Athena." I glanced over my shoulder at where the two demons had been. "What did you do to them?" I stopped and asked the dog.

He sat on his haunches. "When a Guardian or a Warrior touches evil, that's what happens."

"How come it doesn't happen when you touch me?"

"Because even though you're in denial about the goodness in you, you aren't truly evil."

"But I come from evil," I whispered.

"No, you come from both. It's up to you which path you follow." He licked his paw. "That is something I can help you with, though."

"Better yet, why didn't that happen when you bit Ailred?"

"Because he is a low-level demon—his time here is limited anyway. But if I'd held on a bit longer, he may have just perished as well. Who really knows?"

I knelt so I could get eye to eye with the huge dog. "Can I ask you why you chose to come here with me?"

"When my other witch died I could have died with him, but I knew there was more for me to do in this world."

"Wait—so if Rosie were to die, Athena would die too?"

He bobbed his head up and down. "If she chose to. Our mother chose to stay with Alexander when her witch died so she could create us."

"Wow!" was all I could think of to utter.

"We should really try and find Rosie and Athena,"

Ares spoke.

"No, I can't allow that," the demon growled, surprising us.

I jumped, turned, and faced an angry demon. "Ailred, we were just coming to look for you," I lied.

"Sure, you were," he sneered, then pushed me. "We should get going to the next gate before it's too late."

# CHAPTER EIGHT

## *Rosie*

### Third Gate of Guinee

"Come on, we need to get to the third gate. I'm sure Julian is way ahead of us."

Athena followed close beside me and Shay floated ahead of us. As we navigated the labyrinth of tunnels, I saw a figure up ahead. When he turned around a small light to the left of him illuminated his face.

"Julian!" I screamed.

"Wait, Rosie, that's not—!" Athena and Shay yelled in unison.

But it was too late—I couldn't stop myself. I tried to, but my feet wouldn't stop. Athena's teeth bit into my back as she gripped onto my shirt. The sound of material ripping echoed in the dark abyss.

I skidded to a halt, but not before a clammy hand grabbed me. Staring up at the fake Julian, I watched as his eyes turned black. "What the hell? You're a demon.?" I tried to push out of his grasp, but he held on tight. I tried to scream but all that came out was a muffled whisper.

Athena growled behind me, and the demon let me go. My head spun back to look at Athena, who had her jowls pulled back high up over her teeth. Long strings of drool poured from her mouth as she emanated a low growl. She stalked to step between us, the hair along her hackles raised in a ridge along her back.

"Is that a Guardian?" the demon hissed out in my mother's voice. A chill swept up my spine at the fear of this shapeshifting, doppelganger demon.

I slowly turned my head around. When I glanced back at him, there stood my mother who had shrunk back in fear of my Guardian.

"You aren't my mother," I spoke through clenched teeth.

Athena stood beside me. I placed a hand on her back, feeling her hackles rise even more, if that was even possible. For a second, I looked at my Guardian. Her lips were pulled back against her teeth. A thick stream of drool still hung from her jowls. I'd never seen her look so vicious. A low growl continued to emanate from her.

Shay whispered in my ear, "Be careful. Don't let him touch you again."

I didn't bother asking why, I just squared my shoulders and stood straight and confident. "What do you want?" I seethed in anger.

"I want to help you." A smile crept along the demon's face.

Then a bright light lit up all around us. "Leave us, demon!" a commanding voice boomed in the quiet. The demon screeched in horror and disappeared in a puff of smoke.

I turned around, looking for where the voice had come from. I gasped when I saw another figure walking through the black smoke.

He stalked toward me with his hand held out. "You

must be the Rosie I've heard so much about. I'm Guede Plumaj, at your service." He winked at me and took my hand. "What brings you to my neck of the woods?"

Knowing full well he already knew the answer to his question, I figured, why not play along with his games? "I'm looking for my boyfriend. But I have to pass through all the gates correctly." I sighed tiredly, hoping for some pity from the loa, but not totally expecting anything in return.

He let go of my hand and leaned back against the crusty wall, swatting skeletons arms and hands away from him. Without him saying anything I knew what he waited for—my offering. Athena nudged my bag. I pulled it from my shoulder and dug through it. The loa grinned at me, waiting somewhat patiently. He couldn't hide his enthusiasm though and tapped his fingers together.

"Ahh, here it is!" I exclaimed. I pulled out a bottle of rum and a coconut. "Here ya go." I handed him the offerings.

He popped off the top of the rum and chugged about half the bottle, then poured it over his face.

"Burns just like it should. Just the right amount of peppers." He cocked a brow at me before he doused himself in the rest of the liquor.

As he bathed in the rum, I saw the mummified chicken foot hanging around his neck—the one I needed to get for Marie Laveau. He gyrated his body in the sexual way the guede danced. I stood there in awe, mesmerized by his movements.

Athena nudged me. "We should be getting to the next gate."

"I know, but I hate to be rude." I pointed to the gyrating guede.

He continued his sexual movements toward me, thrusting his body to mine. I felt the heat rise up my cheeks as a wave of embarrassment—or was it shyness —washed over me.

Athena nudged between us before he could grab

me in his grasp. "That will be enough," she growled low.

Guede Plumaj grinned widely and stopped. "I shall let you pass onto the next gate. Hopefully, you will find your beau in time." He stopped for a dramatic pause, running his index finger across his lips then sucking on it methodically. I felt my entire body flush, but he continued. "If you can't find your beau, I'll be here waiting." He cracked a smile and held his hand to his heart. "Now you must hurry. I fear he is way ahead of you on his journey," he said as he cracked open the coconut and touched it to his lips. I watched in awe as he gyrated around drinking from the hard fruit.

"Come on, Mom, we need to get going," Athena begged me.

"Okay, but I need something before we go."

The loa was dancing, spinning around and around. When the chicken foot was clearly in my sight, I silently said a little spell.

*Spirits ahead and those behind.*
*Your powers I call for them to align.*
*See now my focus on this object,*
*My possession it must be with no suspect.*
*Powers that bind and flow free.*
*Come to me now and hear my plea.*

I closed my hand around the chicken foot and stuffed it into my bag with the rest of my goodies. I laughed softly and shook my head as the guede danced and sexually gyrated his way down the tunnel, the light disappearing as he did.

"Now we can go." I turned back to face Athena and Shay. We walked a few steps and I dared to look back. I watched with a smidge of satisfaction, as the dark tunnel was devoid of either guede or demon.

# CHAPTER NINE

## *Julian*

### Fourth Gate of Guinee

Another wrought iron gate stood before us, much the same as the others. But this time the details showed the tiny skulls carrying coffins to their final resting place. One little skeleton stabbed another. He scooped up the dead and shoved him into a box. The blood trickled down and onto the knob. Ailred placed a hand on the bloody glass handle and started to turn it.

"Wait, wait." I tried to prevent Ailred from continuing. Part of me feared the agony I would encounter when I passed the threshold of the gate.

He stopped, resting his hand on the doorknob, and faced me. "Julian, why do you persist in delaying this? You're just making it harder on yourself."

"Because." I doubled over once again, but this time the pain lessened. I glanced at Ailred. "Sorry—continue."

He glared. "Why are you in such a hurry now?" His anger peaked.

"No reason."

The demon opened the gate, and we descended the steps. "Hurry up, Julian, we need to get through," he grinned. "You'll get to meet Baron Cimitiere." He turned back and practically skipped ahead in merriment.

"The demon is giddy, and rightfully so, but he should also be scared," Ares told me.

I took a deep breath as I continued past the gate. The pain was getting better. I wondered what the hell was going on with me. I let out a breath and looked down at the dog. "How do you know this?"

"Baron Cimitere is the doorman between the world of the living and the afterlife, guardian of the cemetery gate. He keeps the dead in and the living out. Can't you see it?"

"See what?" I looked around and when my focus became clear. I saw it. We were in a cemetery full of tombs and mausoleums.

Ailred shouted back over his shoulder. "Come on, stop dillydallying."

We followed the demon slowly and came to a cemetery. A bunch of tombs lay scattered in the area.

"What is this?" I asked.

"This is the fourth gate, the home of Baron Cimitiere."

"Where is he?" I asked.

We looked around, and in the distance, leaning against a headstone, stood a tall, skeletal man. The three of us sauntered toward him. The closer we got I saw he wore a hat and tails much like Baron Samedi. But there was an air of pretentiousness about him.

"It is nice to finally meet you, Julian." He smiled a toothless grin.

"Uh, how did...?" I stuttered.

He laughed. "Oh, my boy, it is all over the underworld that you and your lady friend are here." He sauntered over to us. "We so hope the both of you will stay here with us."

"I'm here to stay, but Rosie is trying to save me."

He chuckled. "Save you from this?" He waved his hands in the air. "Why would she want to do that?"

"Because that is who she is."

Ailred interrupted. "Sir, we must be getting to the next gate."

He glared at the demon. "How dare you, low-level demon. I'm having a conversation with my new friend here."

Ailred sulked back and looked abashed at his reprimand.

"Wait a minute, demon—where's my offering?"

A bottle of fine liquor appeared and floated over to the loa. He grabbed the bottle and popped it open. Two glasses appeared out of thin air, and he poured the liquor. "Would you join me for a drink?" He offered me one of the glasses. Baron Cimitiere ignored the demon and faced me with a smile. "Now, where were we?"

For an instant, I quickly thought maybe I could persuade him to help me find or wait for Rosie to get to this gate.

"Julian, do you think that's wise?" Ares bumped me.

"Ahh, could it be? But...." The baron paused, and after what felt like an eternity continued. "A Guardian slumming it down in the underworld." The loa grinned.

Ares growled. "Best not to anger me."

"Is that so, Guardian?" The loa glared at the dog.

"Okay, enough." I stepped between the loa and Ares.

"Come on, Julian, let me just take one bite out of his—"

"No, you may not," the loa interrupted and stepped back. "Be careful, Guardian."

Ares growled. "No, you be careful. You can't hurt me, my magic predates yours."

I stared wide-eyed at the two. "Are you really

threatening the loa?"

Baron Cimitiere laughed. "Oh, it's fine, what he says is true."

"You should be warned to know I'm a Warrior, not a Guardian," the dog growled lowly.

The baron's black eyes grew wide in his vacant eye sockets. "I thought all of you were dead," he said in amazement.

"Not all—I'm the last of my kind," he barked out.

The baron gave a side glance at the dog and kept a wide berth from him, facing me. "So Julian, what is it you want from me?"

"We don't have time—" Ailred tried to interrupt us again.

"Enough from you," the loa bellowed. "I'll have no more interruptions from a low-level demon." Ailred was flung backward, landing in a heap on the ground next to a tomb. His mouth appeared to be zipped shut with an actual zipper.

I chuckled. "Let's leave him be for a while."

"Be careful, Julian," Ares said as I followed the loa.

"Now, what is it you would like from me?"

"I was wondering if you could help me find Rosie."

He shook his head. "All I can do is stall your time here." The loa tipped his hat at me.

# Chapter Ten

## *Rosie*

We walked a few steps and then I stopped. To my right, a flat surface jutted out. I sauntered over to it and sat down. Dropping my head into my hands, I sighed deeply. "What if we can't get to Julian in time? And if we do, how exactly will I save him?" I looked up at Shay. "Maybe I should have waited for my father and the rest of the coven to help me."

"Mom, you know as well as I do that it would have been too late." Athena came over and plopped her head onto my lap.

"I know, but I don't know what I'm doing."

Shay floated over to me and knelt in front of me. "Rosie, if Marie did not believe in you, she would never have gotten me to help you or let you go in the first place."

I looked up at her as she took my hands in hers, even though she was careful not to go through my hands.

"You must believe in yourself and use your inner strength."

"You are right." I wiped away a lone tear that slid down my cheek.

"Good. Now, let's get going and try to get to the next gate."

But before she could stand back up, we heard a deep rumble that shook the walls.

"What the hell was that?" I wondered aloud.

The walls shook then settled some. I held my breath and watched in horror as skeletons dug themselves up from the ground. Once they were topside, they dragged their bodies toward us. I turned around, looking for a way out. From behind me, skeletons grabbed me, clawing at me from the dirt.

"What is going on here?" I hollered over the noise.

As I tried to stand up, I saw Athena struggling with a skeleton who tried to drag her underground. Before it could she dug her back feet in and pulled the skeleton above ground. With a yank, she tugged one of the arms off and tossed it aside. Then she growled loudly as she slung the rest of the bones to the side. The head snapped at her from where it lay and she kicked her back feet at it, covering it with dirt. Yet they kept coming at us.

"What are we going to do? They won't stop!" I panicked. With a wave of my hand, I flung the dead away from me. He or she bounced off the wall and crumbled to pieces.

I looked around to see that Shay was also trying to fight off the dead. We were surrounded by dozens of skeletons, but now it seemed as if fresh dead came at us. The zombies grabbed at us from above as if coming from a somewhat fresh grave. The stench of death overwhelmed me, and I choked, tasting decay on my tongue.

"What is going on here?!" It was as if someone was trying to keep us from moving on. My eyes scanned the dimly lit tunnel, looking for anyone or anything. But nothing seemed amiss.

I stepped forward and raised my hands and started to chant.

*Powers above please hear my plea.*
*An urgent need, I need to flee.*

A zombie ran toward me but fell to the ground. Another tried but I held out my hand and it stopped. I continued my chant.

*A request I make crystal clear.*
*As danger becomes quickly near.*
*The here and now I must escape.*
*Another place I must take shape.*

The dead stopped in their tracks, but not for long. They moved in slow motion until they were no longer under my spell. It was as if someone was controlling them and undoing my words. My eyes went wide, and fear erupted through me.

"Come on, Shay and Athena," I hollered, and grabbed Athena's collar.

We battled our way down the tunnel, tossing and shoving the dead out of our way. Athena snapped and growled as we moved further down.

Up ahead I saw a wrought iron gate. "Come on, let's get to the gate. Maybe they can't follow us down there." I pointed ahead. The lanterns swayed over our heads, threatening to leave us in the darkness.

Shay disappeared and reappeared in front of the gate, waving madly at us as we ran toward her. "Athena and Rosie, hurry!"

The zombies and skeletons shambled quickly behind us, reaching their fingers and hands out to us. We reached the gate and it swung open. I pushed Athena in front of me, taking care to not touch the macabre gate. The skeletons on the iron looked angry.

I followed Athena and slammed the gate behind me, catching the latch on a zombie's hand. It squelched free and flopped on my foot. "Argghhh!" The sound from my throat echoed all around me and I lost my balance.

But before I tumbled backward down the stairs I bumped against my Guardian.

I heard her laugh, then she spoke. "Mom, did you really scream at a zombie's hand like a little girl?"

I regained my balance and turned around. "Yes." I rolled my eyes.

"But you are a powerful witch," she joked with me.

I shrugged. "I still get squicked out over zombies." Then I turned to Shay. "How did you get it open?"

She shrugged. "It was already open."

Before continuing, I sat on a step. "I think someone else is here."

"Why?" Athena asked me.

"Because when I did my spell, it was as if someone else was trying to undo it. I could feel the pull of magic from me as the words came out."

"What do you mean?" Shay floated in front of me.

"It was as if someone was trying to stop my spell. They were working magic against me."

Even as the words came out, I knew in my heart it could only be one person. Gabby. I pushed the thoughts out of my head and hoped nothing else would stop me. Shay, Athena, and I charged down the steps in silence.

# Chapter Eleven

## *Julian*

"I can give you some time, but not much." The baron tapped his chin. "What shall we do to kill time?" His eyes lit up. "I know. Do you know how to play chess?"

"You play chess down here?" I asked in disbelief.

"I do."

Before my eyes, a skeleton appeared. It knelt and held its hands up in the air, then bowed his head. A black and red board floated over and landed, resting itself on the skeletal hands.

"Sit," the loa instructed me, nodding to the other side of the board.

Out of nowhere two leather and wood high back chairs positioned themselves on either side of the board. They were intricately detailed with skulls and snakes. I gazed in fascination at the beauty.

Baron Cimitiere sat with an air of snobbery. He

rested his arms on the leather armrests. He crossed his lanky legs and looked up at me. "Now let's play."

The chair behind me scooted forward, knocking me backward into it.

Ailred stood over in the corner fuming. "Julian, we don't have time for…." But he stopped speaking as his mouth zipped shut. His eyes went wide as he struggled to speak.

"Thank you, Baron Cimitiere," I laughed. "He's getting to be a nuisance."

Ailred's screams were muffled, and his face was bright red.

"Sit, demon," the loa demanded.

In an instant, Ailred did as he was told, though I highly doubted it was his own doing.

On further inspection of the board, I noticed tiny carvings etched into the squares. I couldn't quite make out the designs.

"Do you like the board? It's rather unique, isn't it?" he asked with a grin. Before I could ask what the engravings were, he continued to speak. "The designs are the veve's of the loa."

I nodded and glanced down at the board. On it stood thirty-two pieces resembling tiny skeletons, except for the rooks, which resembled intricately detailed marble mausoleums. In a blur the loa scooped two pieces from the board and held them in his hands, closing his skeletal fists tightly around each piece. Even though his hands were skeletal I couldn't see the pieces.

"Pick a hand." He grinned.

I thought carefully, then pointed to his right hand. He opened it to reveal a red skeleton. The piece leapt from his palm and made its way to its proper place on the board. Then one by one my pieces introduced themselves to me. My king turned around and smiled a toothless grin at me, his top hat a little crooked on his head. Before it could slip off, he tipped it slightly and balanced on his staff. His tuxedo jacket was open at the waist, showing off his alabaster bones. I peered closer, noticing the tiny, beautiful details of each piece.

Then one of my knights removed his helmet and bowed to me, holding his shield and sword close to his body. My queen straightened her back, a red flowing dress wrapped around her skeletal figure. She nodded her head to me. Her crown of flowers never even moved. I was mesmerized by her beauty.

Cimitiere smiled at me. "The queens are beautiful, aren't they, my boy?"

I nodded in agreement.

"All the pieces are representations of the underworld." He waved his hands in the air. "The kings and queens, who are my favorites, of course, represent Baron Samedi and Maman Brigitte."

He waved his hands, instructing the introductions to continue. My two bishops stepped forward, their robes brushing against the chessboard, and bowed at the waist, being ever so careful not to make the mitres on top of their heads waver. The rooks never moved since, of course, they were marble mausoleums of the cemeteries, and finally the pawns. On further inspection, the pawns wore tattered pants and shirts and held tiny guns at their sides. They all tipped their rugged hats in unison. My pieces all had red outfits with black trim, and the loa's pieces had black with red trim.

The loa cleared his throat and the tiny skeletons turned on a dime and stepped back into their respective places.

I picked up the pawn in front of my queen, his little feet dangling in the air. He was ice cold to the touch, and I almost dropped him but didn't. Making my apologies, I gently placed him in the square two spaces up, then waited for the loa to make his move.

He tapped his chin, pondering his move. Then he took his bony fingers and pushed a pawn in and mimicked my move. The little skeleton almost tumbled, but quickly caught himself.

I moved my next pawn another two spots up. After a few moments, the loa moved his pawn beside the other one.

Before I could scoop the pawn up, what happened next caused me to stare in shock. My pawn steadied his gun and aimed it at the other pawn, who in turn held up his hands in protest, but it was too late. The gun went off and the little skeleton slid down, making his death scene a little dramatic. A little pool of blood soaked into the black square. As I watched in amazement the pawn disappeared into ash, which blew away in the nonexistent wind.

The loa just laughed and took advantage of me and slid his bishop in for the kill of my pawn. But this time, the red square began to bubble and then turned to liquid. The little pawn was sucked downwards, gurgling in protest. I pushed my chair back and looked under the board, wondering where he went. "Where did he go?" I noticed my other pawns standing there, wiping nonexistent sweat from their brow. The loa just sat back in his chair and grinned.

I moved another pawn up one, and the loa moved his bishop back. The tiny skeletons danced in their squares.

Neither of us said a word as we moved piece after piece. In our next moves, we both slid our knights onto squares.

The loa reclined in his chair, crossing his lean legs, and steepled his fingers together and rested them under his chin. I leaned forward, contemplating my next move, and finally decided on my pawn, after which his next move was his bishop next to my pawn.

Afraid of his bishop taking my queen, I moved my bishop in front of my queen, who glanced at me in appreciation. But in return he moved his bishop and took my knight. The square bubbled into a liquid, and once again the chess piece disappeared.

"Damn," I muttered under my breath. I slid my final knight over and he shoved his queen forward.

I took his pawn and watched as my pawn once again aimed his gun and shot. The tiny skeleton sunk down, holding his head up trying to breathe one last time. "Wow, these guys sure are dramatic," I said to no one in particular. As I watched him die and turn to dust, finally the little pawn was no more.

The loa chuckled. "They do have a flair for the dramatic." He cocked a brow at me, then moved another pawn forward.

My only play currently was to move my pawn farthest to the right up two spots. He followed by shifting his bishop in front of his knight. My bishop slid beside my knight. Then he moved his one bishop back one space.

He had me in check, so in order to protect my king I moved my bishop back in front of the queen.

"Ah, good move, son."

Then he moved his queen two spaces forward.

I took his bishop with my queen. She reached forward and tightened her tiny skeletal hands around his neck, then squeezed until his head fell off and crashed to the board. His body slumped and quickly disappeared, but the loa took my bishop with his knight. The knight unsheathed his sword and struck the bishop, cutting him in half.

In retaliation, I took his queen with my knight. The little skeleton glanced up at me with sorrow in his eyes then turned around, then in a blink took his sword and sliced the queen's head off. It rolled around the board, finally stopping at the edge where it plummeted, but before hitting the ground it disappeared.

Cimitiere laughed hard. "Good move." He moved his rook beside his final bishop.

Without hesitation, I moved my queen back beside my king. In return, he moved his bishop next to one of my pawns. To save my knight I moved him back over in front of my rook. The loa moved his rook over, so with his next move, he could take my queen. I had to shift my queen over.

Taking his time, his bishop slid back beside his pawn.

Next, I took his pawn with my queen. Without much hesitation and in a blink of an eye, she wrapped her bony hands around his neck and squeezed. His head popped off like a cork from a champagne bottle and flew into the air, then disappeared.

His rook slid in front of his bishop. My rook went two places sideways, and he followed with moving his knight cattycorner to my rook.

By this time, I realized I could nudge the piece and it would walk to the spot I wanted. I scooted my rook one square over. Next, the loa slid his rook four spaces down.

My pawn was next. I nodded at him and he hopped to a square. The loa took a bony finger and pushed his bishop in front of my knight.

My pawn took his bishop, who struggled to remain standing after being shot. In retaliation, the loa took my rook with his rook. My rook crumbled into a million marble pieces.

My queen took his rook. With a wave of her hand, his rook was smashed into a dozen marble bits. Anger etched across Cimitiere's face as he moved his knight backward. He leaned back in the chair and crossed his boney arms and watched with intent as I moved my knight. With a nod of his head, his pawn shuffled into a square.

I leaned forward in thought. "Take it slow, but maybe let him win," Ares spoke in my head. My bishop slid into the square behind his knight. We had him in check, but he moved his king.

I desperately wanted this game to last a little longer but feared it was almost over. So I made a move with my rook to hopefully drag the game out. He followed with a move of his pawn. My knight followed, as did his. He grinned at me.

After a few more moves I finally got to where I could win this game. Since there was no way I could drag it out, I decided to go with my next move. Without hesitation, I moved my queen one space over and grinned at him. "Checkmate," I said, satisfied.

But I hadn't foreseen what would happen next. His eyes turned red and he slammed his hands down on the board. The movement knocked it off the pedestal. The skeleton chess pieces that were left flew up in the air, and when they landed, they skidded and ran into the darkness. The chaos that ensued worried me for the tiny skeletons.

"You should've let him win," Ares told me.

"I know, but I got carried away trying to drag the game out," I sighed.

The loa stood. "Demon, you can take him to the next gate. I want him out of my sight."

# CHAPTER TWELVE

## *Rosie*

The silence was deafening, but there was no gatekeeper to greet us. My thoughts swam around my head, like, why was Marie having me get these items? It had to be something important. But right now, I couldn't concentrate on that—I had to find Julian.

We continued down the steps in silence and came to a darkened tunnel. My eyes darted around, seeing only the dank, fungus-covered walls.

"Shay, shouldn't there be a loa to greet us?"

She nodded. "Yes, there should be."

"Which way now?"

Shay moved her head from side to side, then pointed. "This wa—"

But she never finished. To my horror, she was sucked into the earth. A loud pop resounded as she disappeared.

"Shay!" My screams echoed loudly off the dirt walls. Athena bounded over and barked. Mid-bark she flew backward, disappearing.

"No Athena, come back!" I screamed. When the dust had settled, so to speak, I stood there alone—no Guardian, no spirit guide.

A familiar voice whispered in my head. *Petal, relax and believe in yourself.* I did as the voice instructed.

I sucked in a deep breath and called out to my powers, pulling all my strength from the earth. Quickly bracing myself, I held out my hand and a small ball of light bounced in it. As it moved up and down, I whispered a little spell.

*Words of power against my blocked sight*
*Remove the darkness and bring forth the light*

The ball reminded me of the fairies from the bayou as it danced to and fro. Then my amulet began to burn hot against my chest. I glanced down and it glowed dimly but began to get brighter as the orb in my hand bounced in front of me.

"What—?"

But I was interrupted by evil laughter. From out of the shadows stepped Gabby, her black robe wound tightly around her. Her breasts heaved as she walked toward me. Anger wrapped around me. I knew deep down she was the one messing with me.

"Hello, Rosaleigh." Her face filled with hatred. Her displeasure was laced on the tone as she said my full name.

"What are you doing here?" My anger was evident as I stalked toward her. "Did you get rid of my spirit guide and Athena?" I said through clenched teeth, holding back my anger.

A malicious smile etched across her face. She walked around me, her cloak dragging the ground and stirring up the dirt. I covered my mouth, making sure not to inhale. She stopped and glared at me.

"One question at a time. First, I'm here to see you." She smiled with satisfaction. "As for the other two, yes, I had to get them out of my way.

"What did you do with them?" I demanded.

She twirled one of her ebony pigtails with a perfectly black manicured fingernail. "All you need to know is that they are out of the way so we can talk."

I noticed the hideous snake tattoo remained, but without its head. "Missing something?" I taunted her.

She ran a finger over the snake's body and laughed. "I have vowed to get you back for killing Asp." She rubbed her arm, but the snake didn't move this time.

I sneered. "What do you want?" I crossed my arms over my chest and stood my ground.

"I want payback for this." She growled low, holding out her arm. "I want you to pay for all you've done to me. I want revenge for the death of my mother."

"I've done only what you and your dear mother deserved," I spat.

She stopped circling me and tilted her head. "I knew you had it in you."

I turned around and faced her. "Had what inside me?"

"Evil."

"What? I don't have evil in me." I gaped at her.

Her laugh chilled me to the bone. "How else do you think you can walk down here when you aren't dead? Only the dead belong here." She twirled her pigtail again. "So that must mean you are evil." She sneered at me and waved her hands in the air, the sleeves of her cloak falling to her elbows. "This place is for the dead, but yet you walk freely through here as if you haven't a care in the world."

"I'm searching for Julian. I'm not evil."

"Yes, it's in your blood. And we all know Julian is evil as well."

"Liar!" I screamed.

"Saying it doesn't make it true," Gabby mocked.

"You have no idea what you are talking about. Your jealousy is showing through," I mocked back.

"If you don't believe me, I'll show you," she replied seriously.

She inched closer to me, but I backed away from her.

"Don't worry, I won't touch you." She grinned evilly. "Just watch." She waved her hands in front of me.

Before me a vision began to play, one of my father and another person. I couldn't hear what they were saying, so I inched closer to the hazy vision. Then as a blanket of silence floated over us, I could hear everything clearly.

*"Dominick, you killed him with a spell."*

*My father slammed his fist down on the table. "It was an accident. Someone else messed with the spell and the elixir."*

*"Who?" The woman pursed her lips in disbelief.* I tried to get a glimpse of her but her back faced me.

*"You know who did it." He cocked a brow at her. "Even though I wasn't fond of his wife. Besides, I wouldn't wish any harm on him. I just wanted to stop him from hurting my wife and newborn child."*

*"Yes, but now I fear that you have caused Yvette to lash out. You killed her husband. She will want revenge, and she knows now that you and your family are powerful witches."*

*A little glass bottle sat on what was left of the table. The woman picked it up. "Be careful," my dad said.*

*"I'll be fine. Besides, I can't be killed since I'm no longer of this world." She sniffed the little glass bottle, then put it back down. "Do you have proof that Yvette messed with it?"*

*He shook his head. "No."*

*"Why would she kill her own husband?" the woman asked.*

*He walked away, shaking his head. "Yvette has no love for anyone but herself. You know that. All she cares* about is power," my father said, hanging his head. "Besides, what is the best way to make sure I'm out of the picture?" He paused. "Frame me."

"Then I'm afraid this will have to go before the high council," the woman said.

Instantly shackles appeared around my father's wrists.

"You can't do this, Parmys." My mother came into the room, holding me.

The elder witch shook her head. "It must be taken to the council."

My mother stepped in between them. "You know Yvette did this."

"Perhaps, but there's no proof," Parmys replied, and in a flash disappeared with my father.

When the vision disappeared, I stared back at Gabby. Her mouth was in a horrible grin.

"You see, dear Rosie, your father killed mine."

I shook my head. "No. That's no proof," I growled as I glared at her. "You know it was your mother that killed him."

She shook her head, her grin malicious. "As you've witnessed yourself, there was never any proof."

I planted my feet firmly on the ground. "Where did you send Athena and Shay?"

She laughed and petted the snake tattoo seemingly out of habit. For an instant, I saw sadness cross her face as she realized the snake was dead. Then her expression changed to satisfaction. "I'll never tell you, but you'll never see that damn mutt again. And as for your so-called spirit guide, without her you'll be lost and never find your one true love."

"You bitch!" I screamed, then darkness came over me.

# Chapter Thirteen

## *Julian*

### Fifth Gate of Guinee

"It's about time." Ailred grabbed my hands gleefully. "We are almost to the end of this adventure."

I pulled myself from his grip and sighed deeply. Ares nudged me and I patted him on the head. Even though I'd chosen this, sacrificing my life to save Rosie, I was saddened to realize I'd actually never hold her in my arms again.

I paused, causing Ailred to push me in the back. "Hurry up, Julian, we must get through all the gates."

I sighed, trying to figure out how to keep stalling, but nothing came to me. Maybe when I saw the next loa I could talk to him more.

Ailred walked ahead of me, turning to check on me every so often. The moment I passed through the gate I held my breath, waiting for the pain to come, but this time I only felt a tinge. I ignored Ailred's impatient sighs and looked over at Ares, who walked close to me as if he was meandering through a park or forest.

"Ares, how come you seem so calm?"

He shrugged his head. "I have faith that we'll get out of here, but not before one or two disasters. What's a better question is, how are you so calm?" He nudged my hand where my wolf ring once resided.

"Believe it or not, I'm trying very hard not to shift. I'm afraid if I do, I won't return to myself. I'm surprised I haven't turned already."

"Why?" asked Ares.

"That ring was the only thing stopping me from turning."

"Maybe, maybe not," Ares barked.

"What do you mean?"

"Well, think about it. You've had every reason to turn, but yet you haven't."

Before I could answer Ailred hollered from a short distance away. "Hurry up! A few more feet and we'll be at the fifth gate." He giggled manically.

"Who enters?" A voice boomed in the darkness.

In the dark, I saw Ailred shake a bit. I nudged Ares and whispered, "The demon is scared of this one."

The dog sat on his haunches and licked a paw. "Rightfully so."

"How do you know this?"

"Because this loa is Guede Babaco."

"Very good, Warrior," a voice spoke in the darkness.

"Baron Babaco is the one who can visit dreams."

I gasped. "How do you know so much?"

It seemed the dog literally laughed. "Remember, I'm not your typical dog—I'm magic."

"Is Athena as smart as you?"

"I'm sure she is, but she was a little sheltered since she didn't leave the mansion when the rest of us did."

"What do you mean?" I asked.

"The rest of us left very early on—in fact, a very

long time before Athena was brought here. She had to wait for Rosie to be ready to accept her."

I gasped in shock. "How old are you, Ares?"

Before he could answer me, Ailred came over and stomped on my foot. "Stop talking! You're in the presence of Guede Babaco."

"Ow! You little ass—" I couldn't finish the word as the demon stared at me.

The loa stepped out of the shadows. "Who do we have here?" He sniffed the air. "Ah, a demon and a rougaroux...." That last part drawled out as his lips curved into an evil smile.

"You've heard of me?" Ailred asked with glee.

The loa glanced down at him in disgust. "Everyone knows you are guiding the rougaroux through the gates. Besides, your stench has drifted to each gate. It's almost unbearable to breathe down here." He bent down to his level. "Why don't you go back to where you came from and let me take over?" His eyes sparkled.

I wondered where he'd come from, but my attention was brought back to the two arguing.

"No," Ailred said defiantly, but quickly looked abashed as the loa glared down at him.

I nudged Ares and hid a chuckle. Ailred glared at me, but I quickly turned my attention to the loa.

The loa focused on me. "How may I be of help to you, Rougaroux?" I couldn't think of a way to ask. But he interrupted my thoughts and smiled at me. "You want to see your woman. Am I right?"

I sighed. *Maybe if I kill time here, she'll show up soon.* I kept that to myself.

"Okay, can you show her to me?"

"Sure. But you must be asleep."

He led me over to a dais and instructed me to lie down. I did as he wanted while Ares remained close to me. Within seconds my eyes became heavy, and I couldn't keep them open. The picture started out fuzzy, but soon it was as clear as if she were in front of me. She was slumped over, her legs sprawled on the ground.

I opened my eyes with a start. "What the hell? Where is Athena?" I glanced down at the dog.

The loa stared wide-eyed at me. "How did you do that?" he muttered in disbelief.

We ignored the ravings of the loa.

"I knew they were separated," Ares whispered to me.

"Why didn't you tell me?" I asked angrily.

"Because you have enough on your plate without worrying about Athena."

The loa pulled his attention back to us and gasped. "You mean a Guardian is loose by herself in the underworld? It can't be." I glanced up at him as he seemed to panic. "Maybe you're wrong," he stuttered. "Let's continue this."

The loa waved his hand in front of me and the picture replayed itself. He shook his head as I continued to watch the scene play out in front of me. I didn't even question why I wasn't put back to sleep.

"Athena is nowhere around. She would never leave Rosie's side," I told Guede Babaco." I returned my gaze to the scene, not waiting for a reply.

"Where is—?"

But his next sentence never made it out of his mouth, because I cursed loudly, stopping him.

"What the fuck is she doing here?"

"Who?" the loa asked curiously.

"Gabrielle," I spat out. "She is Rosie's archenemy."

Gabby stepped up and stomped on Rosie's leg. Even from where I was, I heard her scream of pain. Rosie popped her head up and glared at her. She waved a hand and I saw her mumble under her breath. Gabby flew in the air and slammed into the wall. She fell to the ground with a thump.

"Ooh, your girlfriend is feisty." The loa grinned as a chair materialized out of thin air. He sat and leaned forward with a bowl of popcorn, watching the show before us. He popped a kernel into his mouth.

"Where did that come from?" I pointed to the bowl.

"Would you like some?" He offered the bowl to me.

"No, thank you." I waved it away and watched as he returned his focus to the veil. I followed suit.

"This is better in technicolor than in a dream." He grinned. "Would you like sound?" the loa asked.

"Sure, why not?" I grinned hesitantly.

Gabby tried to stand back up, but Rosie waved her hand and tossed her around like a rag doll. Her lips moved, and for the first time, I could hear her. "You'll do to remember I have more power in my little pinky than you do in your whole body." She slammed the witch down on the ground. A loud thud echoed around us. Gabby's black hair was now a mess of half pigtails.

The loa grinned again. "Surround sound."

Gabby flew back up and knocked Rosie backward. "Is that so?" Gabby snorted out.

"Yes." Rosie raised her hand. I could see her lips moving, and I knew she was quietly doing a spell.

Suddenly Gabby dropped to the ground, her legs splayed out to either side of her. She tried to push herself up, but Rosie stopped her with a raise of her hand. I watched as her lips moved and the dirt and walls wrapped around Gabby. Skeletal arms encased her like branches of a tree.

A huge smile crossed my face. "That's my girl."

"That's enough of that," the loa groaned. "You should be going to the next gate."

Ailred grinned widely. "Let's go."

"Before you do...." The loa grinned. "You should find the Guardian before she causes trouble." He looked at Ares. "You know as well as I do that you Guardians and Warriors are not safe by yourselves in the underworld."

"But wait—I thought you could hurt demons," I asked Ares.

"We can, but our power is linked to our witches. Once we are claimed we must remain with our witches in order to maintain our full power. With Athena by herself, she's in danger. She has limited powers."

I looked at Ares in shock, knowing I needed to find Rosie.

"Dear boy, Rosie will be fine. But if the demons find her Guardian, I can't guarantee she won't be hurt." The loa grinned evilly. "We don't want things to get messy down here, do we? And with her being powerful, she'll be a nice, tasty treat." He cocked a brow at me. "Though on second thought, that might be quite a fight to watch."

I gasped, feeling that if I didn't get to Athena before the demons, Rosie would be devastated.

Ailred pushed me. "Come on now."

I glanced over and watched the scene of Rosie disappear. I wanted so badly to hold her in my arms and protect her. I knew she was strong and would overcome this, but if anything happened to Athena.... I shook my head. I couldn't have my sacrifice for Athena go badly. I just had to find her and get her back with Rosie.

"Stop procrastinating." Ailred pushed me forward to the next gate.

# CHAPTER FOURTEEN

## Rosie

The pain in my leg became almost unbearable. A chill went down my spine as I sensed someone watching me. When I looked around, I saw no one except Gabby trying to get out of her prison.

"No!" I commanded angrily.

She struggled under the skeletal arms, but they wouldn't budge. My powers were getting stronger.

Her eyes narrowed at me. "You will never win."

I laughed. "Is that so?" I waved my arms in her direction. "It looks as if I have. You need to learn, and right now, you'll never be as good as me. Good magic will always triumph over your dark magic."

Her eyes sparkled. "Is that so?" Then her face changed to a vacant look and she grinned. "Want to know where your precious Athena and your spirit guide are? If you let me go I'll tell you where I threw them."

I wanted to know their whereabouts badly, but there was no way in hell I would let her out of her prison. I sighed deeply. "Gabby, I know there would be consequences to having you tell me. I can't let that happen. Besides, you lie."

She started to mumble, a spell perhaps.

I stopped her with a wave of my hand. "No, you will not spread your hatred and black magic here." Her mouth shut, and even though she tried to open it, she couldn't. I smiled, realizing that my powers were indeed getting stronger. I'd shut her up with a wave of my hand. I struggled to stand as the pain emanated from my leg. I sucked in a breath and willed the pain to stop. I stepped back and whispered these words.

*The dead to rise to grab and enclose.*
*There you will stay for the time froze.*
*In an earthly tomb held there for now.*
*Magic will hold tight to my vow.*

I watched in awe as Gabby disappeared into the wall of dirt. As my words finished, the earth pulled her back, the dingy alabaster skeletal arms holding her tightly. In seconds she was safely bundled up in the walls of the underworld. A bug crawled around and through her messy hair, disappearing behind her.

Silently I stood, and after a few moments I let out a sigh. Looking around, I started to feel defeated. I didn't know where to look for Athena or Shay. My hatred for Gabby fueled my desire to end her now, but I knew if I went that route I could never come back from it. I already had one kill to my resume. I leaned against the opposite wall and contemplated how to find my Guardian and my spirit guide.

"Damn, how am I going to find them?"

*Petal, let your powers lead you*, my mother's voice echoed in my head. For an instant, I looked around for her, but sadly she was nowhere to be seen. A wave of sadness wrapped around me for a second. Then I pushed off the wall and wiped the dirt from my hands on my pants. "I can do this, Momma!" I said aloud and full of confidence.

I looked one way and then the other. Then I closed my eyes and let the ancestors speak to me. Sucking in a deep breath I remained silent, waiting for the elements to lead me to find Shay and Athena.

After a few minutes, I heard whispers. My eyes popped open, but I stared into nothingness. No one was there and the whispers were distant. I blinked my eyes and closed off to all distractions.

*The powers that be, show my Guardian to me.*

Nothing. I repeated the spell but still no hint of where she was. My heart ached and tears streamed down my face. "Athena, where are you?" I hoped she could hear me. But again, I was met with an eerie silence. Fear reigned inside me as I suddenly thought I would never make it out alive and I'd never see Athena or Julian again. Then I remembered Shay and pulled myself up and, closing my eyes, said another spell.

*The powers above calling far and wide.*
*Send forth to me my spirit guide.*

The whispers started again but this time I could make out what they said. When I reopened my eyes, before me stood my ancestors. The women smiled, their ethereal bodies all holding hands. I saw my mother, and hers before her. They remained silent, then spoke. "Follow us, Rosie."

I held my breath so they wouldn't disappear. Rubbing my hands together, a warm bright ball of light rolled around in my palm. Letting my feet carry me forward, I followed my ancestors. Their ethereal bodies floated above me, leading me left, then right.

I stopped suddenly and held my breath. Up ahead a silhouette stumbled in the darkness. My senses told me this wasn't Shay. I blinked and held out my ball of light, but still couldn't make it out. Hesitantly I kept walking toward it. When it got closer the ball of light bounced ahead. Loudly I gasped when a skeleton erratically walked forward. As it passed me, I pressed my body as close to the wall as I could. It turned and grinned at me with a toothless smile as it made its way down the tunnel. I imagined if it had been wearing a hat it would have tipped it at me.

I released a sigh, then followed the ghosts and turned right, another right, and then a left. In the dimly lit darkness, I tripped but caught my balance by grasping the wall beside me. My hands dug into the dirt-encased barrier. Worms and bugs crawled over my hands, though I didn't dare glance down. I just shook my arms, hoping to get them off. "Ugh," I shuddered when I no longer felt any creepy crawlies on me.

At the end of the long dark tunnel sat a shimmery figure. I ran toward her. "Shay, Shay!" My voice wavered at the excitement and slight disappointment of seeing her. She looked up, and a look of surprise covered her face.

"How did you find me?"

"I said a spell." My voice faltered for a second. "But...."

"What's wrong?" she asked.

"I can't find Athena. I did two spells, one to find Athena and one to find you. But the one to find Athena didn't work. Not that that's a bad thing, it's just...." My voice fell away.

She glanced up at me, her face showing no sign of being insulted. "I understand, Rosie."

I continued, not wanting to hurt her feelings. "It's just that my mother made it so Athena and I would always find each other. When that didn't' work I did a spell to find you." Fear swam though me at the possibility of not finding my Guardian. My ancestors milled around in silence.

"Hmm." Shay tapped a finger to her chin. "Perhaps

she has a cloaking spell on her."

My eyes went wide as saucers. "Oh my goodness. Why didn't I think of that? Gabby is a horrible bitch." I slapped a hand over my mouth. "Sorry for my language."

She chuckled softly. "No reason to be sorry. I'm sure you are right about this person."

"I am. Now to find my Guardian."

I raised my hands and called out to the ancestors and said these words.

*In this moment, please remove the cloak.*
*Clear the air and away the smoke.*
*The path be clear that I must go.*
*The way I must see that you shall see.*

As I finished the words my ball of light glowed up ahead. But I also felt my birthmark warming on my hip. I turned to Shay and smiled, and touched my hip with a finger, the warmth radiating through my skirt.

My mother stepped forward with the others. "Go my child. Find her."

"Thank you, Mother." She caressed my face, then turned away from me. The other women followed her, and they all disappeared.

With my spell working and my birthmark glowing, I knew it wouldn't take long to find Athena. "Come on, let's go." I ran ahead, knowing Shay was right behind me. We followed the light through the underground catacombs, down one tunnel to another.

I had almost lost hope we were on the right track when a huge object ran into me. It knocked me to the ground and started to lick my face. "Athena!" I screamed. Glancing at her chest I saw her birthmark and her amulet glowing a soft myriad of colors. "Thank you, Mom," I whispered. I felt a warmth wrap around me and Athena.

"Mom." She stepped back from me, a bit of drool hanging from her jowls. "Where is Gabby so I can rip her apart?"

"She is in the walls," I replied.

"In the walls?" She cocked her head at me.

"Yes, I trapped her. She won't be getting out anytime soon," I said, not purely sure.

She sat on her haunches. "Mom, we know anything is possible with her. Promise me I can tear her to pieces if she escapes."

I stood up and dusted the crusty dirt off me, not entirely sure what I had just been laying in. "I think I have an idea of what to do with her, but we must find Julian and Ares first."

# CHAPTER FIFTEEN

## *Julian*

As we made our way to the next gate, I contemplated everything that had happened in my life. I nonchalantly kept putting one foot in front of the next. The gas lanterns waved to and fro above our heads, lighting the way.

A chill caught in the air. I shuddered, then a voice spoke. "Julian, do you wish to see your witch?"

"Yes," I spoke to the voice, looking around.

In the distance, a figure stood against the wall. Once we were closer, he pushed off the wall and sauntered over to us.

Ailred gasped loudly and started to bow at the waist. "Julian, you must show respect."

I stopped in my tracks and tried to focus my eyes in the dim light. Out of the shadows stepped a skeleton man. He eyed the Warrior beside me. "You are keeping yourself in check, aren't you, Ares?"

"As much as possible, Baron Samedi." He growled low in respect.

As he spoke to my dog I wondered aloud, "What's the catch?"

Pulling my gaze back up, I stared into a skeletal face. The figure grinned and tipped his top hat. The skulls that adorned it rattled and clanked as they hit each other. He straightened up and held out his hand to me. "Hello, Julian. I'm Baron Samedi."

"May I ask you a question, your...uh...uh...?" I didn't know what to call him.

The loa turned and faced me, leaving the demon angry. His lips curved in a malicious smile. "You want to know the meaning of life?" he teased.

"Not exactly."

He eyed me coolly. "I know you wish to see your witch, or at least stall more in order to speak with her."

I gasped, but before I could answer the loa spoke.

"Oh, come on, Rougaroux. We all know your motives down here." He twirled around and looked at me backward. "We all know you sacrificed yourself for your witch and her Guardian."

He leaned in closer. I sucked in a breath before the scent of death permeated my nostrils.

He pondered that for a moment. "The only thing I can do for you is offer a way to maybe see her."

"Damn it."

"You thought maybe I could transport you to her." He shook his head. "The underworld doesn't work like that. Besides, you are already past those gates. You can't go back unless you want to chance getting lost and stuck in here forever."

I turned my attention back to him. "What is your offer?" I asked, crossing my arms over my chest.

He looked over at Ailred and smiled. "First we need to get rid of him." He nodded his head over to the demon.

I laughed. "I've tried that since he dragged me down here."

Ailred reluctantly stood back up and cleared his throat. "Uh, sir, we have another gate to get to before yours."

The loa never even glanced at the demon—he just kept his focus on me. Then he draped an arm around my shoulder and we walked away from Ailred. I could only imagine the anger emanating from him. Ares stayed close to my side.

"What are you willing to do to see your girl? What if I could make that happen for you?"

I knew deep down there would be strings, but I didn't care. I wanted to feel her in my arms just one more time. "How?"

He grinned widely and tapped a boney finger to where his lips should be. "I have an idea. I need you to solve a riddle for me."

I nodded. "All right."

"If you answer it correctly, I'll make sure you meet up with Rosie. But if you don't, I'll take you directly to the final gate. And there will be no goodbyes to be said."

I shuddered. But seriously, what other choice did I have? Ares pressed himself against my leg.

"I'll play."

By that time Ailred had slunk up near us. "Sir...," he hesitated. "Your Highness."

Samedi never glanced back at him, but spoke. "What is it, demon?" He spoke slowly and clearly.

"Uh, it's just...." He paused, then after a few seconds, he started again. "The rougaroux is...is mine to...to take to the end," he stuttered nervously. He looked abashed after speaking and dropped his head.

The loa petted him on the head then turned back to me, ignoring the demon's words, which I figured was best for him. Who knew what could happen to him if Samedi took revenge for his disrespect? We walked off, leaving the demon there in silence.

"Now, Julian, are you ready?"

"Sure," I replied, even though I really wasn't. I had never been good at riddles.

"All right, here it is."

*All alone shot in the heart but the shot did not kill. How can that be?*
*Eternity in a cemetery. As we are too shall be.*

He paused, waiting for me to answer.

I stopped walking and looked up, trying in earnest to pull this one out. Ares leaned closer to me, trying to give me confidence for this. I tried and tried to think, then like a lightbulb, it hit me. I grinned and smiled at him.

"The answer is, you're dead before you're shot."

He glowered at me, but before he could whisk me off to my true love, Ailred interjected. He grabbed me by the arm and I quickly grabbed Ares by the collar. In an instant, we had disappeared and reappeared, away from Baron Samedi.

Once we had stopped moving, I faced Ailred. "What the hell are you doing? I don't even know if I solved it correctly."

His eyes went dark and he glared at me. "You are mine to take to the last gate."

I shook my head. "Boy, you are going to be in trouble," I laughed.

# Chapter Sixteen

## *Rosie*

### Fourth Gate of Guinee

We left Gabby in her prison and set out to find the next gatekeeper. Shay floated up ahead. Suddenly, a thick blanket of fog covered the ground. I rubbed my eyes and brushed my hand across Athena's head. "Stay close."

"Yes, Mom."

We maneuvered through the fog blindly. As I shuffled through, I held my hands out so as not to bump into anything. But even that couldn't stop me from running into the jagged edge of an old tomb.

"Ow." I rubbed my knee and hopped around. But I knew the inevitable even before I pulled my hand back up. The scent of copper wafted around me. Blood stained my palm, but I didn't have time to worry, so I wiped it off on my pants as best as I could. "Where the hell are we?" I stammered.

"Hello, Rosie," the voice floated through the fog.

I looked around frantically, and off in the distance, I saw him, a skeletal man leaning against a marble mausoleum. He puffed on a cigar, and in his other hand, he held a wine glass. I slowly made my way to him.

"I'm Baron Cimteire." He tipped his hat in hello. "I see you finally made it." He grinned a toothless smile at me. "Your boyfriend was here," he teased. He looked down at Athena. "As was your brother."

"Yes." I breathed out. "Wait...what?" I stammered out. I thought, *Damn, I need to keep moving.* But I glanced over to Athena. She was staring up at him. I swear the loa and Athena had a silent conversation. Then I heard them.

"How did my brother look?" she asked the loa.

"Athena, your brother seems fine. He has been linked to Julian."

"That's good. I was worried. Thank you," she replied to him.

"Okay, enough talking to my Guardian," I said with a bit of jealousy, not worrying about offending him.

"No harm, Miss Rosie. We don't get their kind here. And Ares seems more aloof than Athena." He then smiled at me.

Before he could ask me, I pulled my bag from my shoulder and gave him a bottle of rum for his offering.

"Mind if we have a quick drink before you head to the next gate?"

Hesitating, I started to shake my head. He eyed me quizzically, and I knew in my mind I couldn't deny his request.

"Sure." I meekly smiled, hoping I wouldn't be here too much longer.

A little round table with a black tablecloth appeared before us in the middle of the cemetery. He waved for me to sit. A chair appeared behind me and pushed into me, forcing me to sit. Two glasses popped out of thin air and landed gently on the table. The fog encircled us as we sat. Athena plopped down beside my chair, laying her head on her paws. She groaned softly, feeling my apprehension at having to stay. Shay floated in the air not far from us, keeping an eye on us.

As I sat down, from my peripheral vision I saw something on the ground. It beckoned to me, waving its little skeletal hand. There, hidden in the dirt and grass, lay a little bloody skeletal man resembling what looked like a chess piece. Before the fog could hide it even more, I said a quick little spell.

*Spirits above of air, sea and sand.*
*Know the object I need in hand.*
*Hidden now on sacred ground.*
*Where it lies it must be found.*
*Hear me loud this is my need.*
*To the piece I follow the lead.*

Slowly the tiny piece floated through the fog to land in my lap. The little man held his sword close to his chest and heaved a sigh. This place was beyond weird. I quickly covered it with my hand. The loa glanced up at me and smiled. Somehow, I knew he knew I had it. I wondered why Marie wanted me to be so secretive. It seemed as if they didn't mind me taking the items.

I glanced up and looked at Baron Cimitiere, wondering why he wanted to talk. I waited for him to speak. The eeriness around me sent shivers down my spine.

I decided to speak. "You said Julian was here?"

He nodded his head and leaned forward. He steepled his fingers together on the table. "Miss Rosie, what are your plans?"

"My plans?" I repeated his question.

"Yes. How are you planning on getting Julian out of here? You know deep down this is your fault."

I dropped my head, then picked it back up. "I know. As for my plans, I'm just winging it."

He let out a bark of laughter, startling all three of

us. From the corner of my eye, I saw Shay shimmer out of view, then come back. My Guardian jumped to her feet and barked loudly.

"I'm sorry to have startled you all. But I've never had someone," he air quoted, "'just wing it.' Then again, I don't think we ever had someone in your situation down here." He poured some of the rum into the glasses that had appeared on the table. "Have a drink, Miss Rosie," he offered.

Not wanting to insult him, I gripped it with both hands. I slowly lifted it to my mouth and took a generous sip. It stung my throat as it slid down. I slammed the glass back down, amazed it hadn't broken in my hand. Worry began to spread through me, and Athena nudged me.

The loa smiled. "You know, I think everything may work out for you and your guy. But I hope not, to be honest."

"Why?"

"I'd like another crack at him with a game of chess."

"Really?" I dared to smile. "He beat you at the game, didn't he?"

He nodded. "Not an easy feat."

I stood up. "I must get going if I'm to find him."

"Be careful," he said as he stood from the table and made it disappear. He stuck a cigar back between his nonexistent lips and sauntered off into the fog.

# CHAPTER SEVENTEEN

## *Julian*

Anger swam through me as Ailred pushed me. I was tired of his attitude. Trying hard to push it down, I continued to walk. Ares's huge feet plopped with every step. My thoughts became full of Rosie. "Ares—?" But before I could ask my question, I tripped over something on the ground. I tried to push up, but someone or something pulled me back. "What the hell!" I exclaimed.

Ailred stepped over me. "Stop screwing around, Julian. I'm tired of you trying to stall."

"I'm not doing this," my muffled reply came.

He kicked me hard in the side, releasing whoever or whatever's hold on me. I jumped up quickly and moved over. I glanced down and witnessed a bony hand, I blinked but it disappeared quickly. Without hesitating, or thinking for that matter, I knelt and brushed a hand over the dirt and grass.

Ares sniffed the area and cocked his head at me. "Whatever it was, it's gone." He sniffed one more time.

As I began to stand back up, I was once again kicked in the stomach. I growled loudly, holding my stomach.

"What the hell!" I looked over as Ailred aimed at me again.

"Julian, I will not tolerate you stalling any longer."

I stood and glowered. "I won't tolerate you kicking me again."

"Is that so?" he smirked.

I stood there, letting my anger consume me.

"Julian, don't," Ares barked out.

But it was too late, I felt the hair creep along my arms. I couldn't stop it. The pace at which I turned was terrifying—I'd never changed this fast before. It had to be this place causing it. Fear wrapped around me like a blanket. But as the creature took hold of me, I no longer felt like myself.

Before I could stop myself I stalked toward the demon, who was a few inches shorter than me. I stared down at him and growled loudly. Spittle hit his face as I pulled my lips back over my teeth. For once I saw fear in his expression. In a low guttural voice, I leaned forward. "I've had enough of your bullshit and your constant bullying. What should I do with you?"

In an instant the demon grinned, gaining some confidence and taunting me. With a smirk, he spoke. "I was doing my job. This is your girlfriend's fault, not mine."

"What did you say?" I picked him up. He was now eye to eye with me.

Fear was apparent once again, but this time in his voice. He sputtered, "Please don't hurt me."

I grinned a toothy grin. "Why not?" My voice was no longer my own—it belonged to the creature. "You've been a thorn in my side since you dragged me down here."

Without a second thought, I took the demon by his

throat and squeezed, feeling a slight satisfaction.

"Julian, stop," Ares spoke.

I turned to stare at my Warrior. I tried to stop but couldn't. The creature wouldn't allow it—my dark side had taken over. I kept squeezing until the demon's head fell backward in my hand. I dropped him and he flopped to the ground.

A low growl emanated from me. "No, but it's your fault you're a dickhead," I said to the dead demon. I kicked him, returning the abuse he'd done to me. My anger started to recede, and I howled loudly in pain.

"Calm down, Julian," I heard the dog coax me. "Change back."

I howled in pain and slumped to the ground. "I'm trying," I breathed out between my clenched teeth.

Ares came over and put his head in my lap. It amazed me that he wasn't scared of me in this form. As the dog comforted me I slowly began to change back to my human self. Once I was a hundred percent me— or so I hoped—I sobbed. "Ares, I didn't want to do that no matter how much he irritated me. Now we are destined to be stuck here forever." This time I was careful not to get angry at myself. I took deep even breaths.

Ares cocked his head up to stare at me. But before he could say anything a voice spoke.

# CHAPTER EIGHTEEN

## *Rosie*

### Fifth Gate of Guinee

Shay glided ahead of me. My thoughts swam inside my head of Gabby and Julian. Would Gabby get out of her prison? She was powerful enough, after all. And Julian...would I get to him in time?

My spirit guide turned and smiled at me. "We are almost there, Rosie."

Athena and I started to walk faster. The tunnel was brighter than before, and up ahead we saw the gate. The delicate designs of little skeletons sleeping in coffins were stunning.

Shay stopped as I looked at the designs. She smiled. "Guede Babaco is the loa who can visit in dreams."

I sucked back a breath. "I can do that."

Without hesitation, I opened the gate, quietly so as not to wake the skeletons. But as it creaked I panicked.

The coffins began to open and little skeletons climbed out. They began to fight each other, drawing blood, which seeped along the wrought iron and spilled over the glass knob. I let go of the it as if it was hot and quickly scooted through it. Athena followed suit, tucking her tail between her legs as a skeleton reached out for her.

When we were all on the other side I wondered if Julian had made it to this gate. It creaked as if no one had been through it in forever.

Athena bumped into me. "I know what you're thinking, Mom."

Shay waved us down the spiral stairs. "Hurry up, girls," she urged, her voice motherly.

We descended. "Is that so?" I smirked at my dog.

"Yes. You are thinking that Julian hasn't made it to this gate."

I nodded. Hope had filled my heart—maybe we would see him after all.

"Well, we should ask the gatekeeper, shouldn't we?"

I grinned down at the huge dog. "Yes, smarty," I chuckled.

Once we had gained access to the next level, Shay and I glanced around in search of the next keeper of the gate. Up ahead I watched a skeletal man dancing around. "There he is." I pointed. He gyrated to the sounds of drums. We all walked toward him.

"Hello, Rosie," he said without even turning around. Finally, after he finished his dance, he spun around to face me. He gasped. "Ahh, you found your Guardian."

The dog cocked a head at him, but I spoke. "How did you know she was missing?" My curiosity was swimming.

He laughed. "Your beau was here, and we watched you kick...." He paused. "What was her name?"

"Gabby," I said in bewilderment.

"Ah yes, that was her name."

My mood fell as I realized Julian had indeed already been here. My heart sank, and I felt sick to my stomach.

"Are you alright?" the baron asked me.

My gaze fell on him and I nodded. "Sure," I mumbled.

I remained motionless for a few seconds then realized he was waiting for his offering. I slowly shrugged my backpack off and dug into it. My heart hurt, and it took me a while to find his gift. Finally, my hand found something and I pulled it out.

He grinned from ear to ear, but he held his giddiness back. Quickly I handed him the bag of tobacco. He took it and opened it up and sniffed with his nonexistent nose. "This is the good stuff," he murmured.

"I'm glad you like it." My head was somewhere else. I wanted to ask him about Julian. My heart begged me to, but my mouth wouldn't work. I opened and reopened my mouth, but it was as if cotton stuck to my tongue, drying it up.

Athena nudged me. "Ask him, Mom."

The guede looked at us. The three of us stood there waiting patiently.

"Do you have questions for me, Rosie?"

I nodded, moving my tongue around my mouth trying to work some saliva through it. I held a finger up to hold on one sec and reached into my bag. Pulling out a bottle of rum, I twisted the top off. Quickly I drank from it, and once I was done, I cleared my throat and spoke. "Can you show me where Julian is?" I asked nervously.

He eyed me. "Are you sure you want to see him?"

Nerves swam through me at a fast pace. "Yes," I stuttered out.

"Okay, but you must be asleep. It's the only way."

I had an inclination he might be lying, but I needed to see if Julian was all right.

He led me over to a marble dais and helped me up.

Athena barked, "Mom, are you sure about this?"

I nodded, not daring to chicken out. I waved my dog over and held on to her collar as she stood beside me. Shay hovered overhead, keeping an eye on the loa.

He stood at the head of the dais and waved his hands over me. "Now Rosie, think of Julian and only Julian."

I did as he instructed, making Julian my only thoughts. My eyes got heavy and I felt Athena place her paws on the edge of the dais. My eyes closed, and a hazy scene appeared before me. Then it became clear.

*Guede Babaco held his hand out to me. "Come, Rosie."*

*I grabbed his hand and followed. I could hear a dog barking in the distance. I looked around but didn't see Athena or Ares. I began to worry.*

*"Don't worry," Babaco spoke. "We are in your dreams. Athena is still beside you."*

*We walked down a long, dimly lit tunnel. My eyes became accustomed to the darkness, lit by a single gas lantern. Off in the distance, I saw two figures. I blinked once, then again.*

*"Julian!" I slapped a hand over my mouth. The anger on Julian's face scared me. But he no longer looked like the man I loved. He was the creature he never wanted to be.*

*I looked up at the loa, who stood beside me. "What's going on?" I asked.*

*He shook his head, then told me. "Watch."*

*I swung my head back to Julian and the demon. Beside him stood the huge blue dog. Even though I couldn't hear him, I knew Ares was talking to him.*

*Then in horror, I watched as Julian squeezed the demon's neck until the demon went limp.*

"Nooo!" I screamed and jumped to a sitting position on the dais. I scrambled off and looked around. "We must get to Julian."

"What happened?" Shay and Athena asked in unison.

I shook my head and willed the tears to not come down. "Julian shifted and killed a demon."

The loa spoke. "Yes, but it was only a low-level demon. Nothing to fret about."

"That's not what I'm worried about, If Julian murders someone he will forever be doomed. Even with his witch side protecting him," I sputtered out between sobs. Guilt swam through me. If he'd never come down here this wouldn't have happened.

"Mom, please don't worry about him. My brother will make sure he's okay."

The loa cocked his head at me. "But he's destined to be here forever, so your worry about him is moot."

My head whipped around to face him. "Yes, I'm very well aware of that. But I'm trying to—" The look on the loa's face stopped me. "I'm sorry for my disrespect." I nervously smiled at him.

"It's quite all right, Rosie. I know this must be harrowing for you to lose someone you love." The loa returned the smile. "It's been my pleasure, Rosie. Please be careful on your journey."

Before we left something by the dais caught my attention. On the ground sat a skull with delicate tattoos etched across the entire thing. Geez, I had almost forgotten to get this item.

The loa followed my gaze and smiled. He walked over to the skull and scooped it up. "Do you like it?"

"Yes. Would you be open to letting me have it?"

He pondered my question, then nodded. It quickly disappeared and I felt something move in my bag.

"Thank you." I smiled, thanking him, and followed Shay to the next gate.

# Chapter Nineteen

## *Julian*

### Sixth Gate of Guinee

We looked around but saw no one accompanying the voice. Slowly I began to shift back. The hair disappeared, first on my hands and arms, then slowly from my body, till once again I was a man. I dropped my head into my hands. "What in the hell am I going to do?" I shook my head. "I killed someone."

"You killed a demon," Ares said.

"Not a person," the voice from earlier said. A skeletal man stepped out of the shadows. He wore the same garb as the other barons but looked somewhat different. When I looked past him I saw what looked like another cemetery, though this one seemed different, as if the burial plots had been dug up. And there were no headstones.

"Who are you?" I asked.

"I'm Baron Kriminel, loa of what your people call

purgatory. Nice to meet the infamous Julian, the Rougaroux." His hand rested on staff much like Baron Samedi's.

I choked out a laugh. "I highly doubt I'm infamous."

He barked out a laugh. "You could be though if you'd let the creature take over before it's too late." He muttered something under his breath I could barely hear. "I'm afraid it may be too late after all." He turned his attention back to me. "Do you have an offering for me?"

Panic wrapped around me, and with my head hung low I stood up. "I'm sorry, but I don't have—"

Ares interrupted me. "We might have something." He pointed with his paw to the dead demon.

The loa passed a glance over to the demon slumped on the ground.

"Will that do?" I asked hopefully.

He nodded. "This time I'll take him since he was murdered." He grinned at me.

I nodded in appreciation. The loa waved a hand and Ailred's body floated over to him and landed on the dirt in front of him. "He was a nasty little fellow, wasn't he?" the loa grinned at me. Not waiting for me to answer, he continued, "The lower-level ones always are. Well, he'll be a fine specimen, and live the rest of his life as my servant."

The loa raised his hands high over the dead body and chanted something I couldn't make out. Ailred's eyes popped open. He stirred and his body moved, unlike anything I'd ever seen.

I muffled a gasp. "You can't," I protested.

He glared at me. "It's my offering. I can do as I please."

Ailred's body stopped moving, then rested on the ground. After what felt like an eternity, he stood up, not looking at me but at the loa. "How may I serve you, my lord?" His voice was monotone and without emotion.

"Please go dig a hole." He handed him a shovel.

With a perplexed shake of my head, I asked, "Why did you send him to dig a hole?"

He barked out a laugh and his hat almost toppled off his head. He winked at me, catching the falling hat. "It's better than that. He'll be digging the same hole for a while. Now let's talk."

"What would you like to talk about?" I inquired.

"You."

"What about me?"

But he ignored my question as Ailred came back up to him.

"What are you doing back so soon?" He glared down at the demon.

The demon shook his head and trudged back to his work.

The loa shrugged his shoulders. "It's so hard to find good help. But back to you."

I waited to see if the demon would interrupt us again, but he didn't. "What is it that you want to know?"

He tapped a bony finger to his alabaster chin and smiled. "Was the demon the first thing you killed?"

I sighed. "Yes, why?"

"And have you been experiencing any pain when walking through the gates?"

"Yes, why?" I asked again.

His expression changed quickly, and he ignored the question. "You should be getting on your way to the next gate." He practically pushed me through it.

# CHAPTER TWENTY

## *Rosie*

### Sixth Gate of Guinee

We all walked quietly, and I gasped in horror as we came across the wrought iron gate. Little skeletons danced in a macabre fashion, killing other skeletons. "How utterly disturbing," I said. Shay nodded in agreement. The blood, as with all the other gates, dripped and colored the doorknob, turning the glass red. I turned it, careful to remove my hand quickly so as not to let any of the skeletons touch it.

We walked through and continued until we entered a cemetery. A skeleton man danced around freshly dug holes, and a figure stood beside him still digging. The gatekeeper gyrated to and fro, tipping his hat at all the graves, a big smile on his white skeleton face. Over his shoulder, he held a sack. With one hand he would wave and grab something, popping it into the bag. I blinked as I witnessed a tiny wisp of white peeking out of the bag. When I looked closer it looked like an incomplete person.

"Shay, what is that?" I pointed to the white hazy blob.

"A soul," she said with a shudder.

"A soul?" I said.

"Yes, Baron Kriminel keeps the souls he takes in that bag."

I shuddered and let out a breath.

The figure with a shovel continued to dig beside him. He looked familiar. "Hey, I thought Julian killed him," I whispered to Shay and Athena.

The skeleton man waved us over, tipping his hat in hello to us. The three of us meandered over to him.

"Be careful, Rosie, this loa should be feared," Shay whispered.

"Who is he?" I pondered.

"Baron Kriminel. He is a known murderer. In fact, it's said he was the one who killed Guede Nibo."

I nodded. "Sure," I said nervously.

"He must be respected as much as the other ones," she told me in a whisper as we reached him.

A belt of severed heads moved with his gyrations. He dropped the sack he was holding.

"Hello, Miss Rosie. Your beau just left," he said rather giddily.

"He did?" I gasped. "Was he okay?" The words tumbled out in nervousness.

The loa glanced over at the demon but then turned his attention back to me. The demon shuffled over to us. "Get back to work," Kriminel demanded. Before heading back the demon looked at me, devoid of emotion.

"Hey, I thought Julian killed him."

Baron Kriminel spun his head to face me. The skulls adorning his hat clacked and clicked as they hit each other. "How do you know he killed him?"

"The gatekeeper before you showed me," I replied.

He shook his head in disgust. "Damn Baron

Cimitiere, always showing off his parlor tricks." Then he laughed. "Though we all have our own ruses down here." He winked at me, which was unnerving with him having no eyes.

Athena snorted and he glanced down at the dog.

"Ah, another Guardian, I see."

"My brother is a Warrior," she replied, wagging her tail.

"Is that so?" He eyed her. "Is there a difference?" But I don't think he actually expected a response. He just stood there staring at me.

I stared back at him, then did a mental forehead slap. "I'm so sorry. I forgot your offering." I slung my bag from my shoulder and dropped it to the dirt. Without looking up at him, I could feel perspiration bead down my back. Then I pulled a small box out and handed it to him.

"Ah, Rosie, what have you to offer?" he said as he ripped the lid off, throwing it to the ground. His hand reached into the box. As he pulled it out, he stuffed the rum cake into his skeletal mouth. "Rosie, this is absolutely divine," he said through bites.

"I'm glad you like it. It was my mother's recipe." I smiled.

He stuffed the last bite into his mouth, then wiped it with a handkerchief he pulled out of his breast pocket. "I have one question for you before I allow you to pass. And you must answer correctly."

I nodded, fearing the question.

He cleared his throat. "Have you ever murdered someone?"

I sucked in a deep breath and slowly let it out as he stared at me. "Yes, I have."

"Did they deserve it?"

I nodded. "Yes."

"Miss Rosie, I shall let you pass." He smiled mischievously.

I nodded and started to walk away toward the last gate. I needed to get one of his severed heads without angering him. With my back to him, I silently said a spell.

*Powers above and powers near.*
*Gather round, I need you here.*
*A missing piece, a part of a whole.*
*Separated the body and soul.*
*A dangling head kept as a prize.*
*My possession a must is my cries.*

The head landed in my hands with my back to the loa. I chanced a glance to see if he noticed, but he had returned to his dancing near the graves.

# Chapter Twenty-One

## *Julian*

### Seventh Gate of Guinee

Without Ailred, Ares and I made our way to the final gate. My heart was heavy. Dread swam through me. I would never see Rosie again. I willed my feet to stop, but I knew if I didn't follow through with this another demon would come for Rosie and Athena.

When we reached the edge of the path, water lapped against the edge. We waited patiently, not saying a word. I could see bodies with their hands raised above the water, their mouths open, screaming in pain. Before I could ask Ares a question I didn't know if he would have an answer to, a pirogue floated through the water toward us. The boat was unique, unlike any I'd ever seen before. The bow had the head of a skeletal alligator, and the stern had a tail. It whipped the boat around to the port side.

Baron Samedi stood atop a wooden seat, dressed

in the finest tails, his top hat adorned with a dozen or so skulls that clacked when he bowed at us. He held a scythe with a skull that included eyes, which glowed a bright white. I was in awe.

The gator's head turned to me and snapped his alabaster jaws. His eyes were blinding white, glowing in the dark. His tail moved in unison, making the boat sway a bit.

"Come aboard, Julian." Baron Samedi motioned to me.

Before entering the boat, I looked down at Ares. "I'm sorry to have brought you here."

"Julian, this is not your fault, and nothing is final. Besides, I chose my fate," the dog said.

I ruffled his ears and he leaned into my touch.

We both stepped into the boat. Baron Samedi placed a hand on my shoulder. "How are you faring?" the loa asked with compassion.

I shrugged. "As good as I can—you know, with the consequences."

He cocked his head at me. "You know, Julian, once you get to your final destination you will be dead."

I spun to face him, horror etched on my face, though I knew what he said to be true. I nodded in agreement and held back the tears. But this had to be done in order to protect Rosie. My hand instinctively petted Ares. He once again leaned into me. I had seen Athena do just the same thing to Rosie. Part of me wished the dog hadn't chosen this fate. I dared a glance up at the loa, but he remained stoic.

"Are we ready?" It wasn't really a question. "Do you have my payment?" He held out his hand.

I panicked. I had nothing to pay the ferryman. Before I could say this, the sweetest voice echoed around me.

"Julian...!" Rosie hollered.

I whipped my head around just in time for her to fling herself into my arms, practically jumping into the boat. Her body pressed into mine, and for a moment we were melded into one.

"Ahem." The loa cleared his throat.

She slid down my body, caressing it softly. I had to hold in a moan. Athena remained on the dock, flanked by the woman I'd seen with Rosie.

Rosie looked up at Baron Samedi and smiled. He still had his hand held out. Her face was grief-stricken at first, but she soon recovered.

"I'm sorry, but Julian can't go with you."

He let out a loud chuckle. "Is that so, Miss Delacroix?"

She hid her fear of the loa well and stood her ground. "Yes."

"I'm sorry, but he must. We must have repayment for your indiscretion," he said with a toothless grin.

"But if you remember, that was your fault—you allowed me to skip all the other gates." She sounded confident in her declaration.

His expression grew angry for a split second, and then he grinned, lifting his hands palm up in a shrugging motion. "Everyone knows I am a trickster." He kept his stance. "Again, I think this is your fault. It would also be wise to not blame me." He glared down at her. "Now we must get going. If Julian doesn't have payment he will end up in the bayou of lost souls."

My gaze went to the water, where people moaned in pain and heartbreak.

"Then take me," she stammered.

"No!" I demanded. I turned her to face me, grabbing her shoulders in both of my hands. "You can't do this, Rosie. You have so much to live for."

"But I can't live without you," she whispered, wiping her eyes. The tears trickled down her cheeks.

I held on to her and peered into her eyes. "You can go on, but I need to do this to protect you." I placed a hand over her heart. "I'll always be with you."

Athena sat on the deck and watched us. Somehow I figured she was having a private conversation with her brother.

I turned my focus back to Rosie. "Please let me go."

"I can't!" She shook her head.

"Rosie," Baron Samedi interrupted us. "I will let you come with us to give you extra time with Julian, but only if you have payment."

She glanced up at him, tears staining her face. Then she dug into her jeans pocket and pulled out my wolf ring.

"How did you get that?" I gasped.

"Easy. She stole it," Baron Samedi answered for her. He held out his alabaster hand. Hesitating, she finally dropped it into his palm. "That will do fine," he grinned. The loa closed his fist around the ring. "One more thing—the dogs must stay here. Your spirit guide can stay here with them."

Rosie looked panicked but remained calm. "No! I've compromised on Julian, but I'll need both dogs, plus Shay." She placed her hands on her hip in defiance.

He shrugged and nodded his head. She waved Athena and Shay onto the boat.

# Chapter Twenty-Two

## *Rosie*

The boat ride was silent. Athena and Ares sat beside each other having a secret conversation. Shay floated above the boat, careful to remain near us. I leaned my body into Julian's and relished in his touch. I didn't want to lose him. How could this be happening? I glanced off into the distance and watched the thousands of souls screaming and trying to grip at the boat. Every time one did Baron Samedi would hit them with his scythe.

Silently we weaved in and out of what looked like a swamp, but darker than the ones I'd known. We floated underneath huge cypress trees, their tendrils of Spanish moss waving and grabbing at us as we made our way. The cypress knees jutted out from the water. I gasped as I watched the white alabaster bones of a skeletal alligator slide into the stagnant water. The palmettos parted as the gator left his perch. His tail swished through the water—he was on the hunt.

"Where is he headed?" I pointed to the alligator.

Baron Samedi laughed loudly. "They eat the lost souls."

Just as he finished his words, the reptile opened his maws wide and his jaws captured a soul. As the dead tried to get away, the alligator took it under the water to drown. The water splashed as the reptilian rolled his prey. Just as quickly as he had attacked it grew silent. I feared what else may be in the water.

Up high in a tree crickets chirped their praise to the alligator. On the bank sat a couple of white bullfrogs. But on closer inspection, I noticed they were skeletal as well.

"Is everything dead here?" I asked.

He smiled over at me. "Why, of course, my dear. this is the underworld." He waved his hands in the air. I held onto Julian.

Suddenly Ares and Athena began to bark. My head whipped around, and I saw it—a black silhouette trying to get into the boat. Ares pawed at the water.

"No!" screamed the loa.

"What's going on?" I demanded.

"The dogs should never have been allowed to come along," he spoke out harshly.

Ares whined loudly and held up his paw. Blood dripped from it onto the bottom of the boat.

"Ares!" Julian hollered. "What has happened to my dog?"

The loa glared. "He's touched the water of the bayou of lost souls. The souls are hungry. A Warrior is like a steak dinner to them."

"What will happen to him?" Athena questioned.

Ignoring her, the loa motioned Ares over to him with two bony fingers. He hobbled over to him, holding up his paw. The loa touched it and the dog shivered. Blood dripped from it as Baron Samedi held it in his skeletal palm. The loa breathed on it and the blood slowly began to stop.

"I thought you were smarter than that, Ares."

"I may be, but I'm also here to protect my witch."

"From the lost souls?" the loa chuckled.

"You can never be too sure," the dog barked.

Once it was merely a trickle, the loa stuck one bony finger to it, and when he pulled back the blood had stopped. The loa grinned at the dog. "Now go sit by your witch," he said.

Ares crawled over to Julian as if he had been scolded. Julian pet him but then doubled over in pain.

"Julian, what is wrong?" I glanced up to the loa, but he remained stoic. "What is wrong with him?" I cried out.

"It will only last a little while longer," Baron said angrily.

Julian slumped over and I held his head in my arms. Athena slowly crawled toward me.

"We are almost there," Baron Samedi spoke.

"Mom, he'll be fine."

I nodded and started to say a spell.

"No!" Baron Samedi stopped me. "You can't."

I turned to him. "Why not?" I demanded.

He sighed. "Damn it, Rosie, can't you just do as I ask?"

I stood, letting Julian's head rest on Ares's back. "Why should I?"

The baron huffed and sighed again. "The reason he's in pain is because his rougaroux side is dying."

I gasped loudly. "Are you serious?"

He rolled his eyes, which was creepy as hell. "Yes, now can we continue?"

"What happens when we get to where we are going?" I asked but was ignored.

The boat continued on its way until we reached a place that looked familiar. I gasped. "This is the end."

The loa nodded. "Now, everyone out of the boat," he demanded.

We all exited, and Julian drew in deep breaths with every step. "You're going to be okay," I said.

"Of course he is," Baron Samedi agreed. "He just needs to let the rougaroux die."

"Then what?"

"Then you go home."

"What?" I screamed at him.

The loa grinned at me and twirled his scythe as it turned into his staff. "You all go home. We have our payment for your indiscretion."

Just then Julian cried out in pain as his rougaroux part leapt from his body. Baron Samedi cast it into the bayou of souls, where it screamed in pain.

"Now, Julian, you have about a quarter of it left as a reminder of who you are."

Before he could answer the walls and ground shook. I turned to face Gabby. "How the hell did you get out?" I screamed.

"Bitch, I'm way more powerful than you ever will be," she spat.

"In your dreams," I retorted.

I raised my arms and pushed her backward, but she stopped midway, then rushed toward me. She wrapped her hands around my neck, her expression full of hate.

"Get your hands off me," I choked out. I tried to pull her hands from my neck.

Julian came up behind her, but before he could pull her off me she waved him off, throwing him against the dirt wall. Both dogs lunged at her with their teeth bared. Without taking her hands from my neck she sent the dogs flying backward, bouncing off the wall. Shay ran over to them to check on them.

I silently said a spell and her hands loosened from around my neck. When I was able to breathe, I brought my hands up from the ground, pulling on all my powers, sending her flying to the edge of the embankment to the bayou of lost souls. She looked over to me and brushed her messy hair away from her face, the anger etched across it. She crawled toward me, chanting something in another language.

Suddenly I understood her.

*Spirits of darkness*
*Hear my call*
*Upon her a trance must fall*
*Her mind blank of all before*
*Her emotions, memories, personality no more.*

Before I could retaliate, she stood and raised her hands. My body spiraled up in the air.

"Gabby, stop this—you'll be sorry."

"No, you'll be sorry. See you on the other side." She grinned evilly as she tossed my body into the bayou of lost souls.

I screamed and fell into the murky, stagnant water. As I sank the last thing, I saw was Gabby smiling, then disappearing into a puff of smoke.

# Epilogue

## *Julian*

My voice seemed foreign as I screamed. I ran over to the edge of the water. It was surreal as I watched Rosie descend into the water. Her brown hair fanned around her as she disappeared out of sight.

Athena crawled on her belly over to me. She howled in pain as she witnessed her witch disappearing. I went to reach into the water, but Baron Samedi stopped me, wagging his finger. "No!"

"But I need to get her out!"

"You can't. You need to go home."

I shook my head. "No. I can't leave without Rosie," I argued.

"Julian, she's gone. Here, give this to Marie Laveau, she'll know what to do with it." He removed a skull from his staff and handed it to me. And then with a snap of his fingers, we all were transported topside.

I spun in circles and dropped to the ground, trying

to dig into it. "Damn it! Damn!"

"What's happened, son?" a voice spoke from behind me. I turned to face Marie Laveau, tears in my eyes. "Where's Rosie?" she asked.

"Gone."

"What do you mean, gone?"

"Gabby threw Rosie into the bayou of lost souls."

She gasped. Athena slumped to the ground and howled. The voodoo queen walked over to her and knelt. "It will be all right." She petted her and leaned in, saying something to her that I couldn't hear. She turned to me and asked. "Do you have her backpack?"

Ares meandered over with it his mouth. "Here, Baron Samedi gave me this to give to you."

"Thanks. Now get the dogs back to the house and let Dominick and the others know what happened."

*To be continued...*

# LISTS OF BOOKS

## Voodoo Vows
Magical Memories
Voodoo Vows Book 1
Black Magic Betrayal Book 2
Spellbound Sacrifice Book 3

## Voodoo Vows Short Stories
Ghosts from the Past
Ghosts from the Present

## The Guardians a Voodoo Vows Tail
Bred by Magic Book 1
Gifted by Magic Book 2

## The Cresent City Sentries
Stone Hearts

## Bayou Kiss Series
Summer's Kiss

## A Legacy Falls Novella
An Unexpected Hero

## Beasts of Atonement MC
The Gryphon's Revenge Book 1

# The Brotherhood of Redemption
The Protector's Kiss Book 1

# Mystical Mansion
Mystical Mortality Book 1

# The Clover Chronicles
Finding a Leprechaun Book 1

# Coming Soon
Trapped by Magic
Stone Player
Autum's Kiss
The Bear's Redemption

# ABOUT THE AUTHOR

As a young girl, Diana Marie Dubois was an avid reader and was often found in the local public library. Now you find her working in her local library. Hailing from the culture filled state of Louisiana, just outside of New Orleans; her biggest inspiration has always been the infamous Anne Rice and her tales of Vampires. It was those very stories that inspired Diana to take hold of her dreams and begin writing. She is now working on her first series, Voodoo Vows.

**Website**:
www.dianamariedubois.com

**Facebook**:
https://www.facebook.com/diana.m.dubois

**Goodreads**
:https://www.goodreads.com/author/show/7690662.Diana_Marie_DuBois

**Instagram**:
http://instagram.com/dianamariedubois

**Pinterest**:
http://www.pinterest.com/dianamdubois/

**Twitter**:
https://twitter.com/DianaMDuBois

**Tumblr**:
http://dianamariedubois.tumblr.com/

Made in the USA
Columbia, SC
16 September 2022

66831210R10072